UP NEXT...

W9-BJQ-186

on **Sports Illustrated** KIDS

:02 *SPORTS ZONE SPECIAL REPORT*

:04 *FEATURE PRESENTATION:*

FULL COURT PRESSURE

FOLLOWED BY:

:50 *SPORTS ZONE POSTGAME RECAP*

:51 *SPORTS ZONE POSTGAME EXTRA*

:52 *SI KIDS INFO CENTER*

ZACK FULLER FACES FORMER TEAM THIS SATURDAY WHEN TIGERS FACE BULL... **SIK** *TICKER*

SPORTS ZONE

PECIAL REPORT

BL
KETBALL

NT
BALL

KT
ARDING

SL
BALL

KY
EY

FULLER'S FORMER TEAM AIMS TO EMBARRASS HIM ON COURT

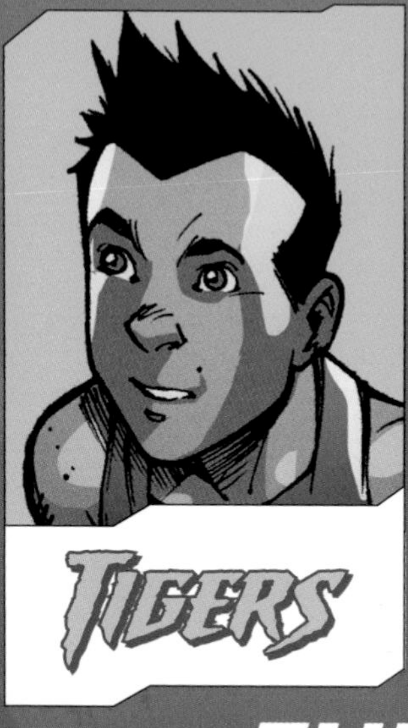
TIGERS

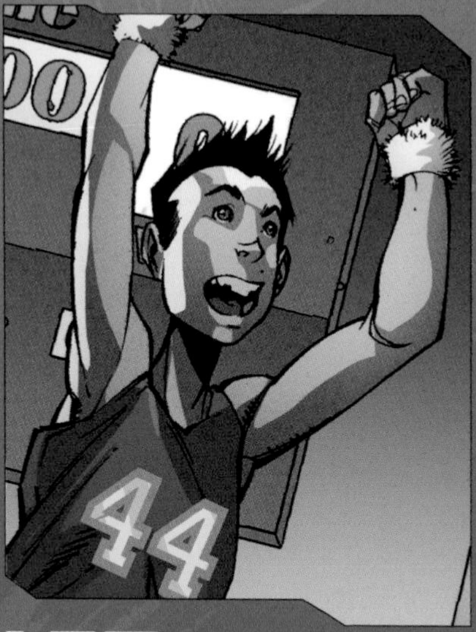
44

ZACK FULLER

STATS:
TEAM: TIGERS
AGE: 13
NUMBER: 44
POSITION: SMALL FORWARD

BIO: Zack is a defensive specialist. He averages 3.5 blocked shots and 2.75 steals per game, and always guards the opposition's best players. But Zack's former team, the Bulldogs, are coming to town, and they think Zack's a traitor for joining the Tigers. To make matters worse, Zack will have to guard his former best friend, Joey Jacobs, who is an ultra-quick sharpshooter.

Sports Illustrated KIDS

UP NEXT: FULL COURT PRESSURE

BLZ vs BKS 3-1
TGR vs RDR 33-32
EAG vs BAN 14-7
SPA vs WLD 4-3
BAN vs RDR 21-15
RZR vs LIG 4-3
BLZ vs BKS 3-1
TGR vs RDR

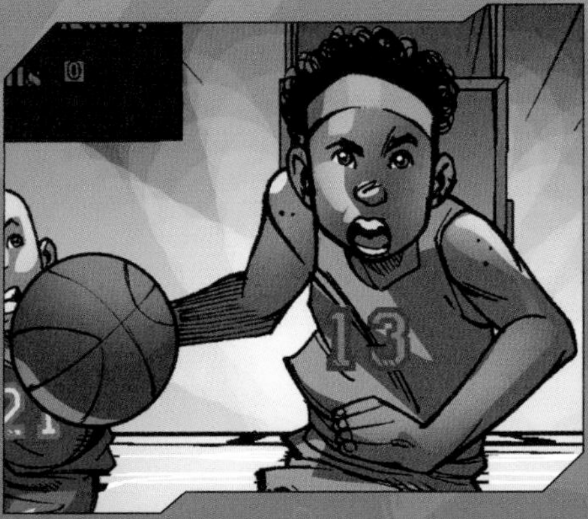

JOEY JACOBS

TEAM: BULLDOGS
AGE: 14
NUMBER: 13
POSITION: POINT GUARD
ROLE: TEAM CAPTAIN

BIO: Joey Jacobs may be the most difficult player in the league to guard. He loves to draw fouls with his lightning-quick head-fakes so he can get to the free-throw line, where he hits nearly 90 percent of his shots. Joey will be out for revenge against his former friend, Zack, when his Bulldogs battle the Tigers.

PERRY BOYD

TEAM: TIGERS **AGE:** 14 **NO:** 77 **POSITION:** SHOOTING GUARD

BIO: Perry Boyd is the Tigers' team captain and top playmaker. When this streaky shooter starts sinking shots, the points begin to pile up.

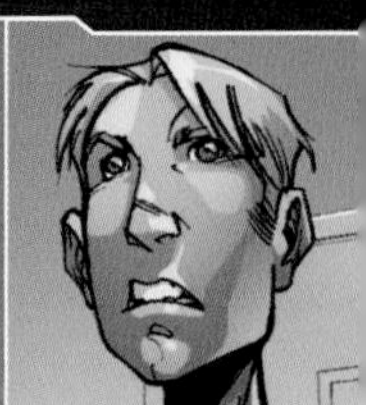

BOYD

ALFONSO HECTOR

TEAM: TIGERS **AGE:** 46 **POSITION:** COACH

BIO: Alfonso Hector is a no-nonsense coach who has a knack for bringing out the best in his players.

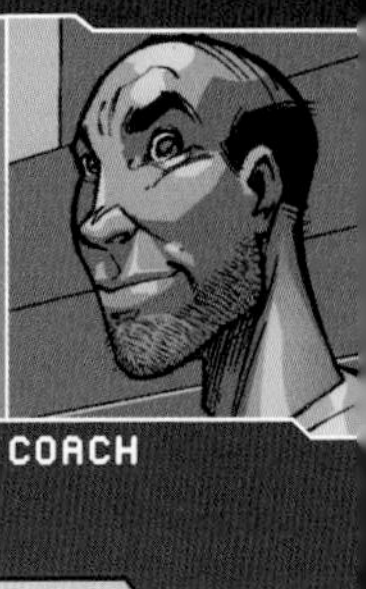

COACH

COACH HECTOR LOOKS TO USE FULLER'S KNOWLEDGE OF FORMER TEAM TO TIGE

SIK TICKER

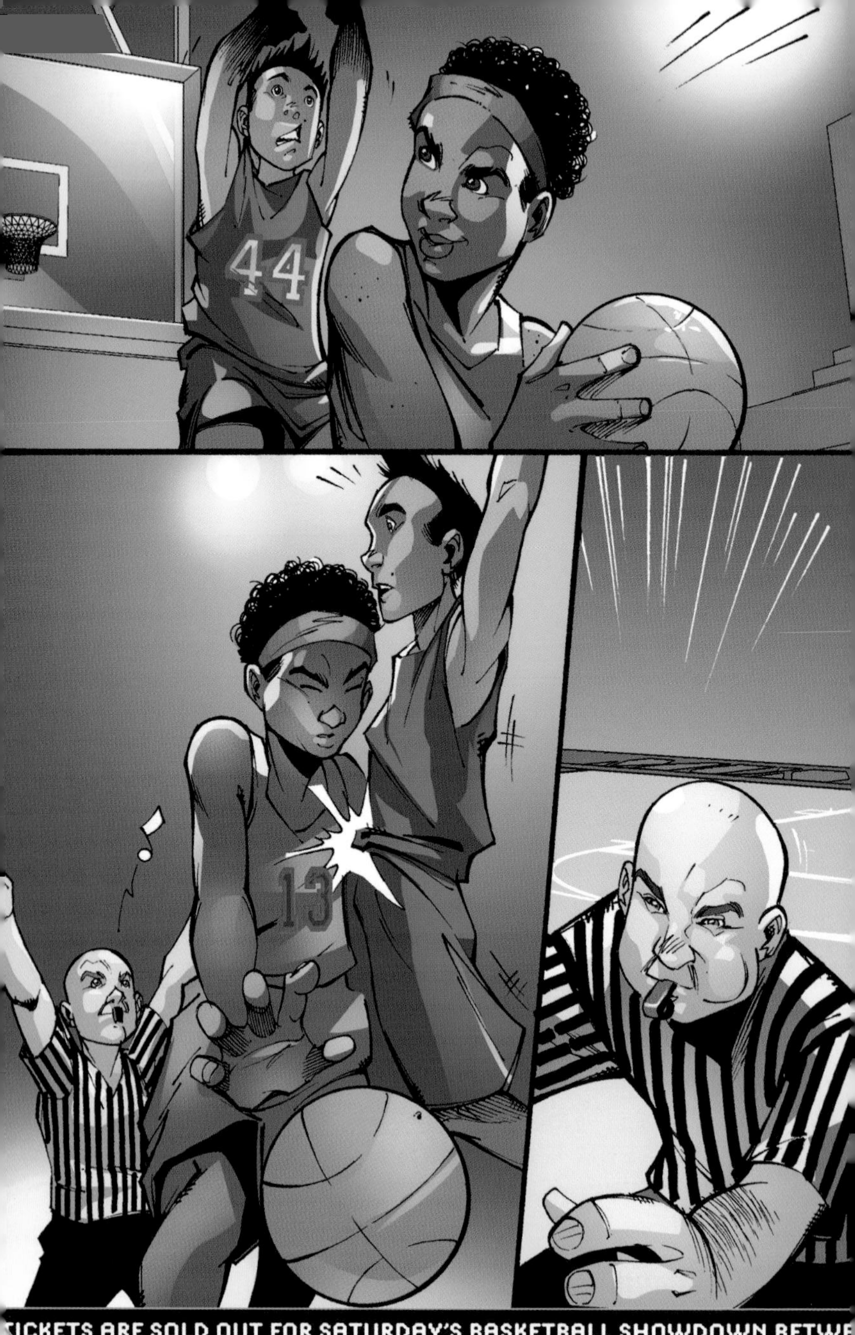
44
13

TICKETS ARE SOLD OUT FOR SATURDAY'S BASKETBALL SHOWDOWN BETWE

Sports Illustrated KIDS

PRESENTS

FULL COURT PRESSURE

A PRODUCTION OF

⚏ STONE ARCH BOOKS
a capstone imprint

written by Jessica Gunderson
illustrated by Alfonso Ruiz
colored by Jorge Gonzalez

designed and directed by Bob Lentz
edited by Sean Tulien
creative direction by Heather Kindseth
editorial direction by Michael Dahl

Sports Illustrated Kids *Full Court Pressure* is published by Stone Arch Books,
1710 Roe Crest Drive, North Mankato, Minnesota 56003.
www.capstonepub.com

Summary: Star defensive player Zack Fuller is in a tough spot. His new
Tigers teammates don't trust him. The players on the Bulldogs, his old
squad, think he's a traitor for leaving. When the two teams face each other
in the playoffs, Zack has to guard his former best friend. To make matters
worse, the Tigers captain refuses to pass the ball to Zack. Caught between
a Tiger and a Bulldog, and in serious foul trouble, Zack will have to find a
way to play through the pressure.

Cataloging-in-Publication Data is available on the Library of Congress
website.

ISBN 978-1-4342-1911-4 (library binding)
ISBN 978-1-4342-2291-6 (paperback)
ISBN 978-1-4342-4946-3 (e-book)

SHARP-SHOOTING TIGERS AND THE ULTRA-AGGRESSIVE BULLDOGS

SIK TICKER

Printed in the United States   5040

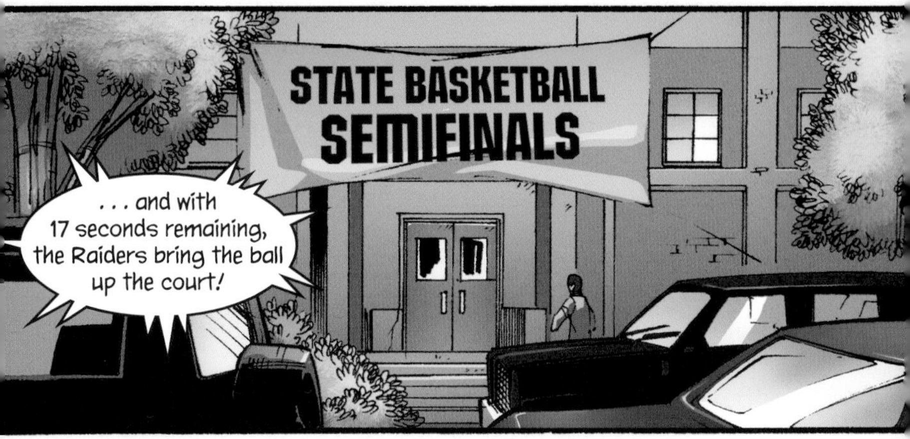
STATE BASKETBALL
SEMIFINALS
. . . and with 17 seconds remaining, the Raiders bring the ball up the court!

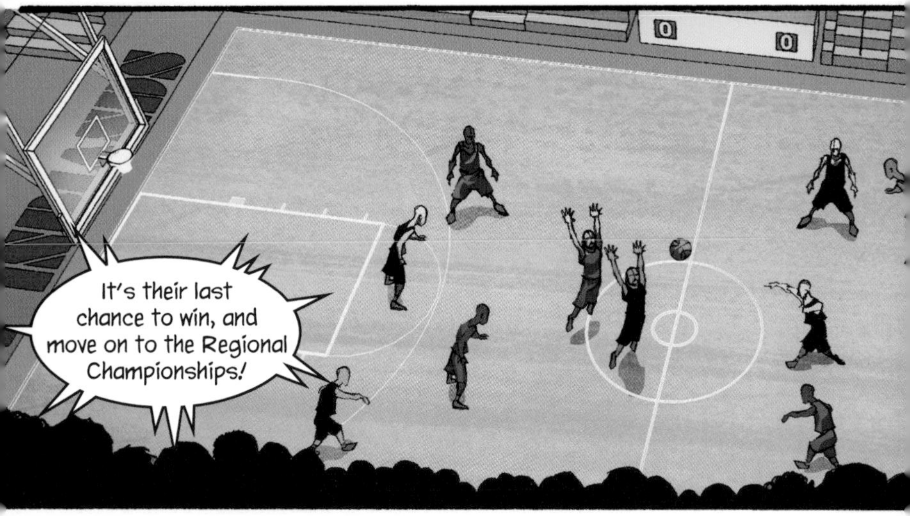
0
0
It's their last chance to win, and move on to the Regional Championships!

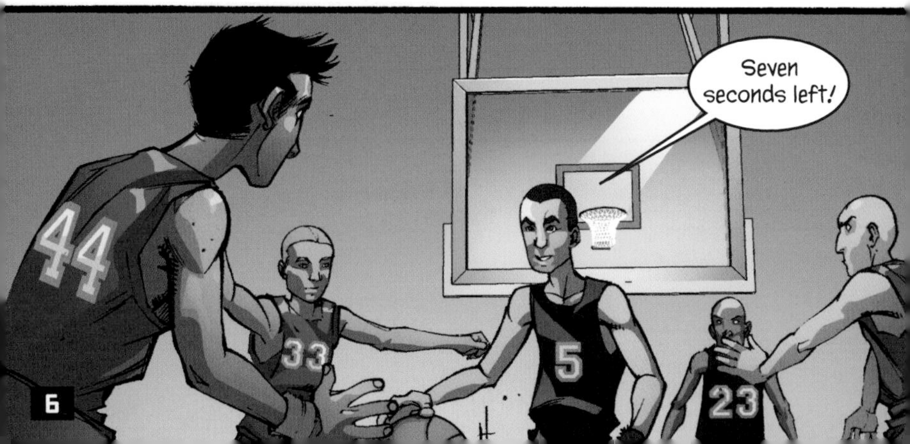
Seven seconds left!
44
33
5
23

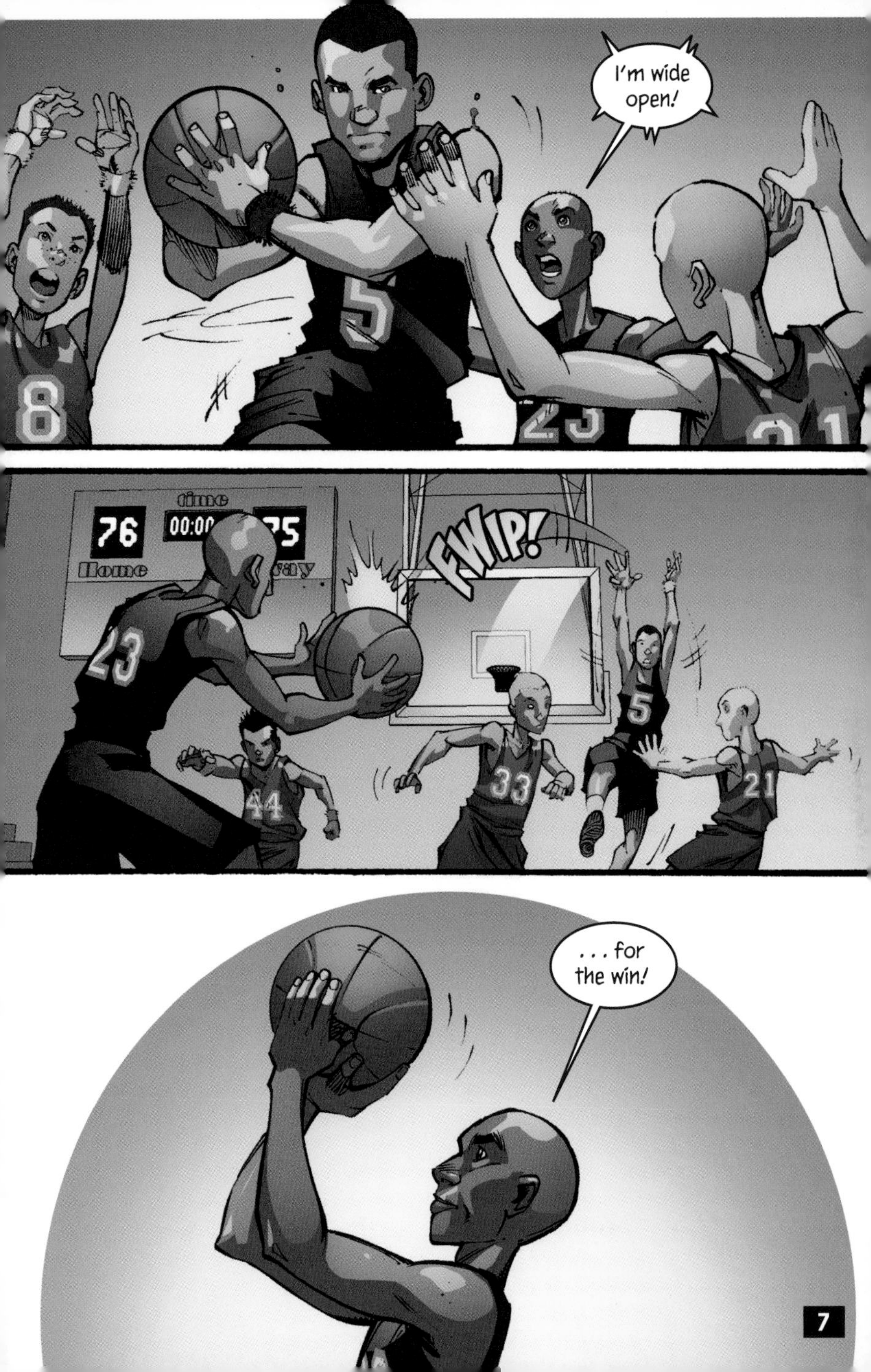
I'm wide open!
76
time
00:00
Home
FWIP!
. . . for the win!

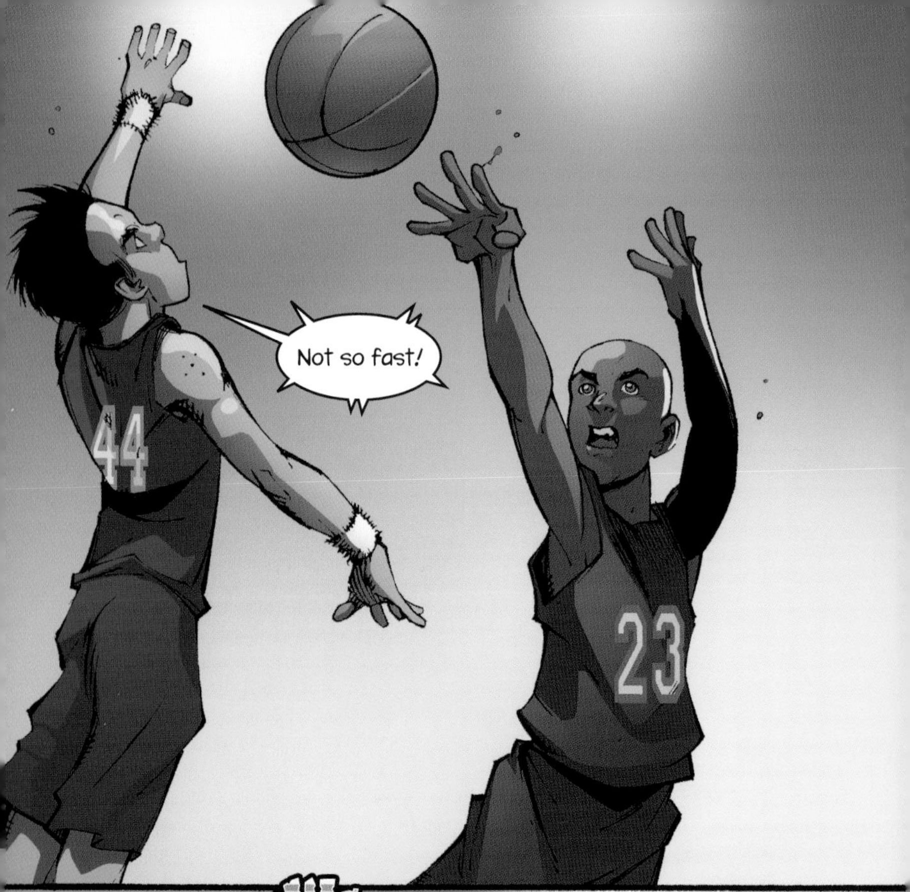
Not so fast!

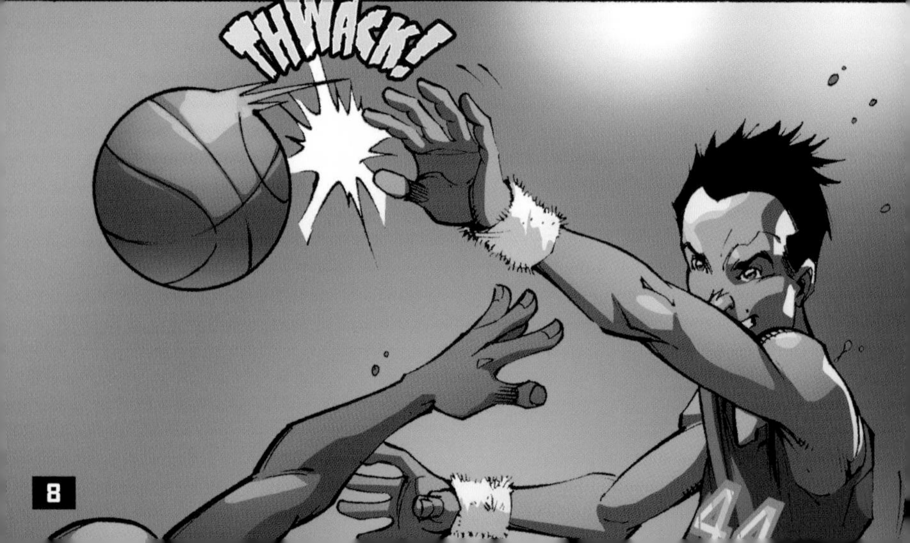
THWACK!

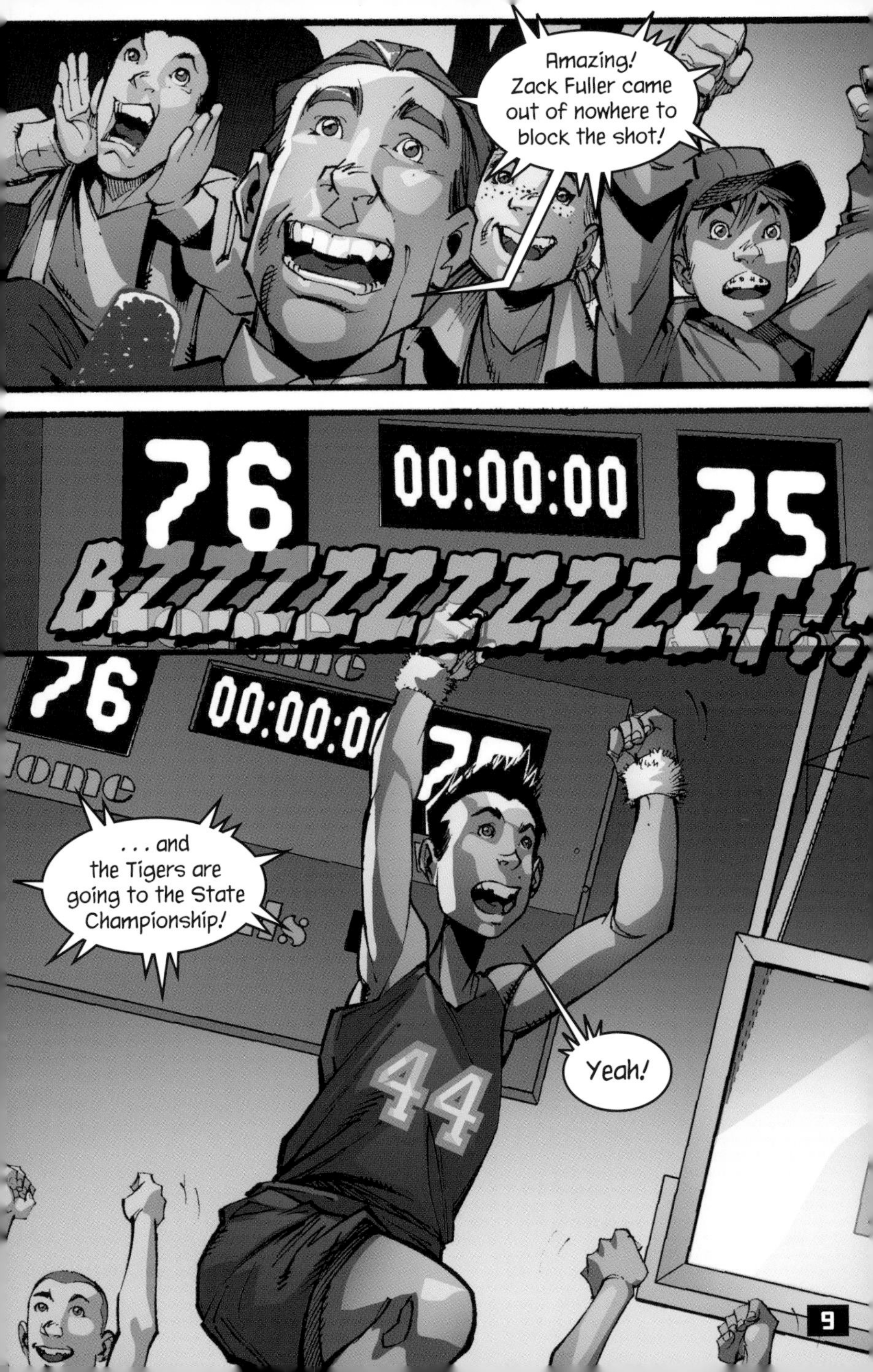
Amazing! Zack Fuller came out of nowhere to block the shot!
76
00:00:00
75
BZZZZZZZZZZZT!!
. . . and the Tigers are going to the State Championship!
44
Yeah!

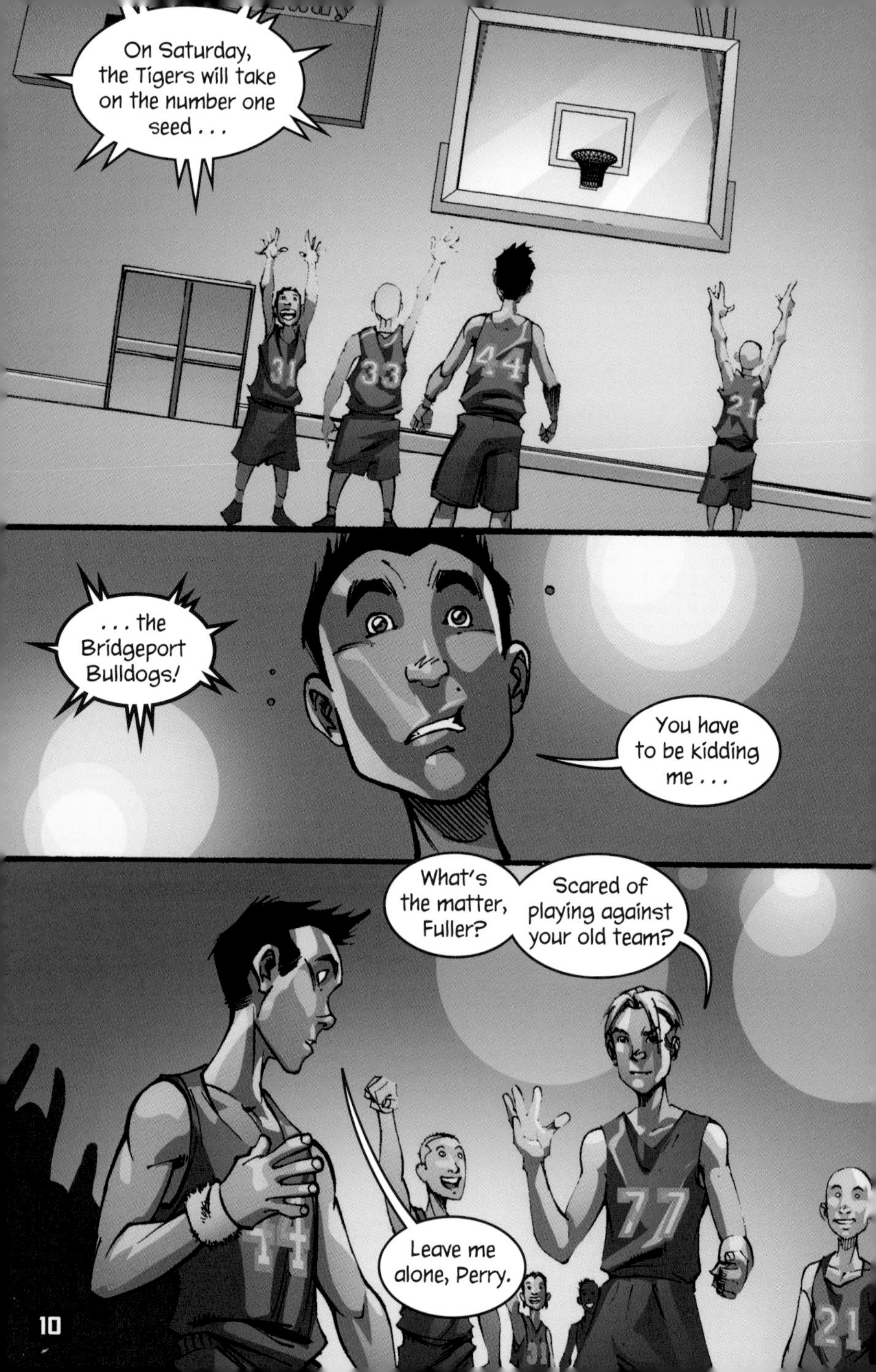
On Saturday, the Tigers will take on the number one seed . . .
. . . the Bridgeport Bulldogs!
You have to be kidding me . . .
What's the matter, Fuller?
Scared of playing against your old team?
Leave me alone, Perry.

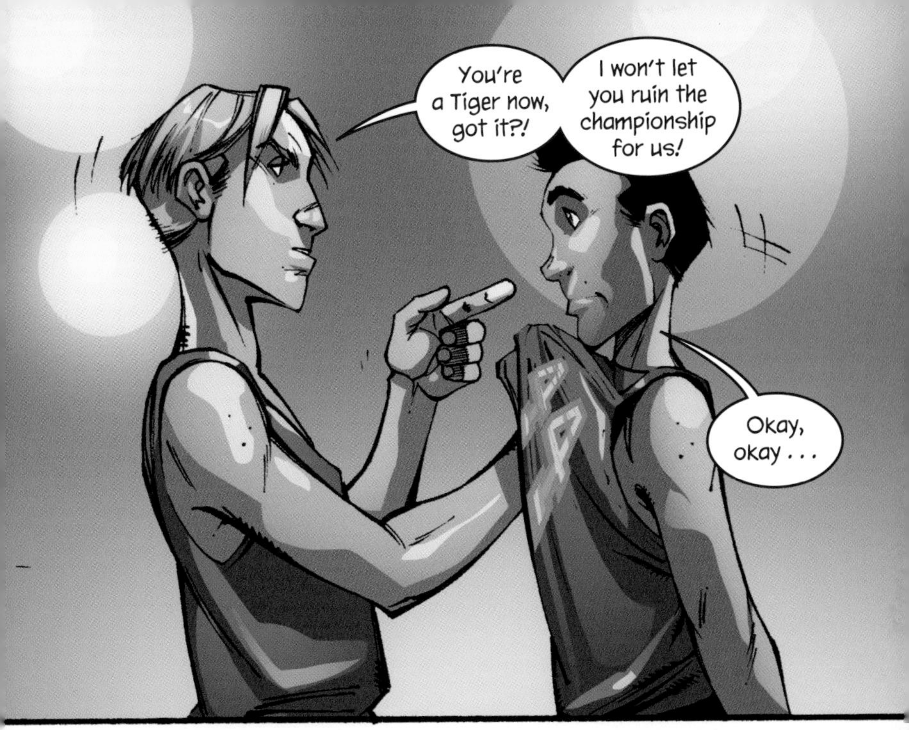
You're a Tiger now, got it?!
I won't let you ruin the championship for us!
Okay, okay . . .

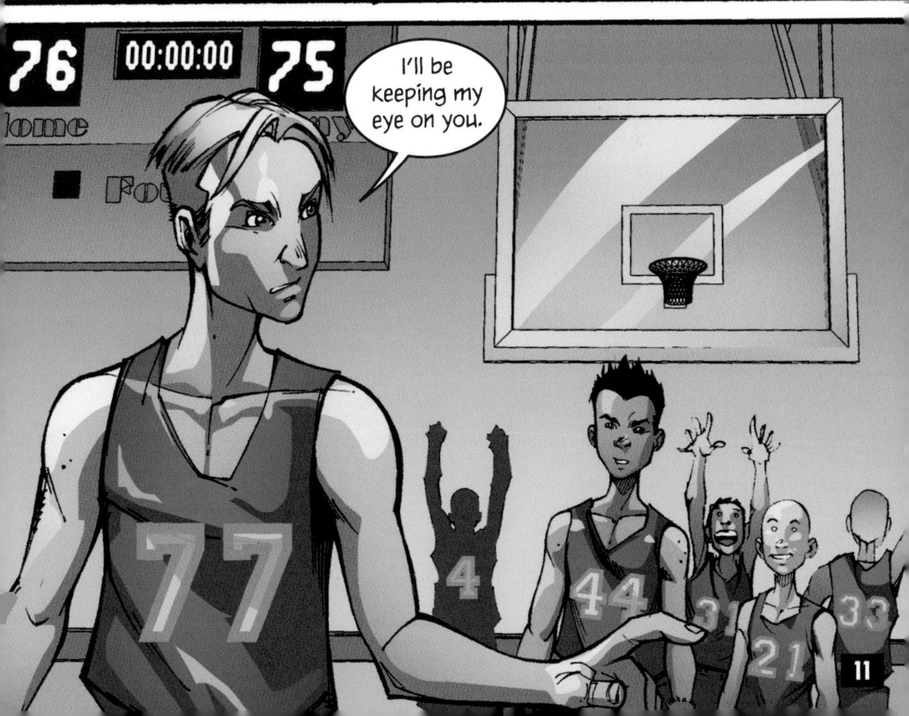
76
00:00:00
75
I'll be keeping my eye on you.

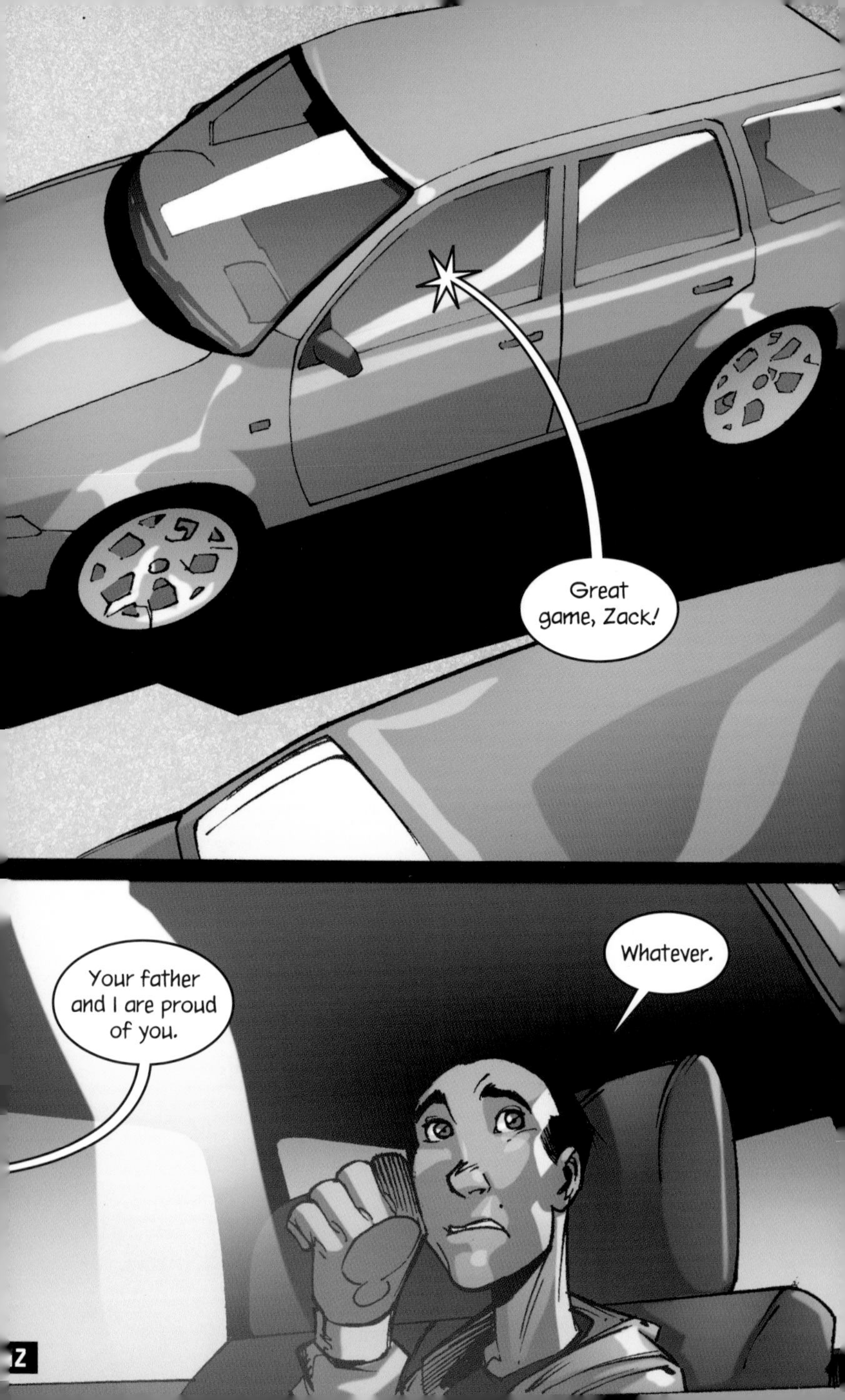
Great game, Zack!
Your father and I are proud of you.
Whatever.

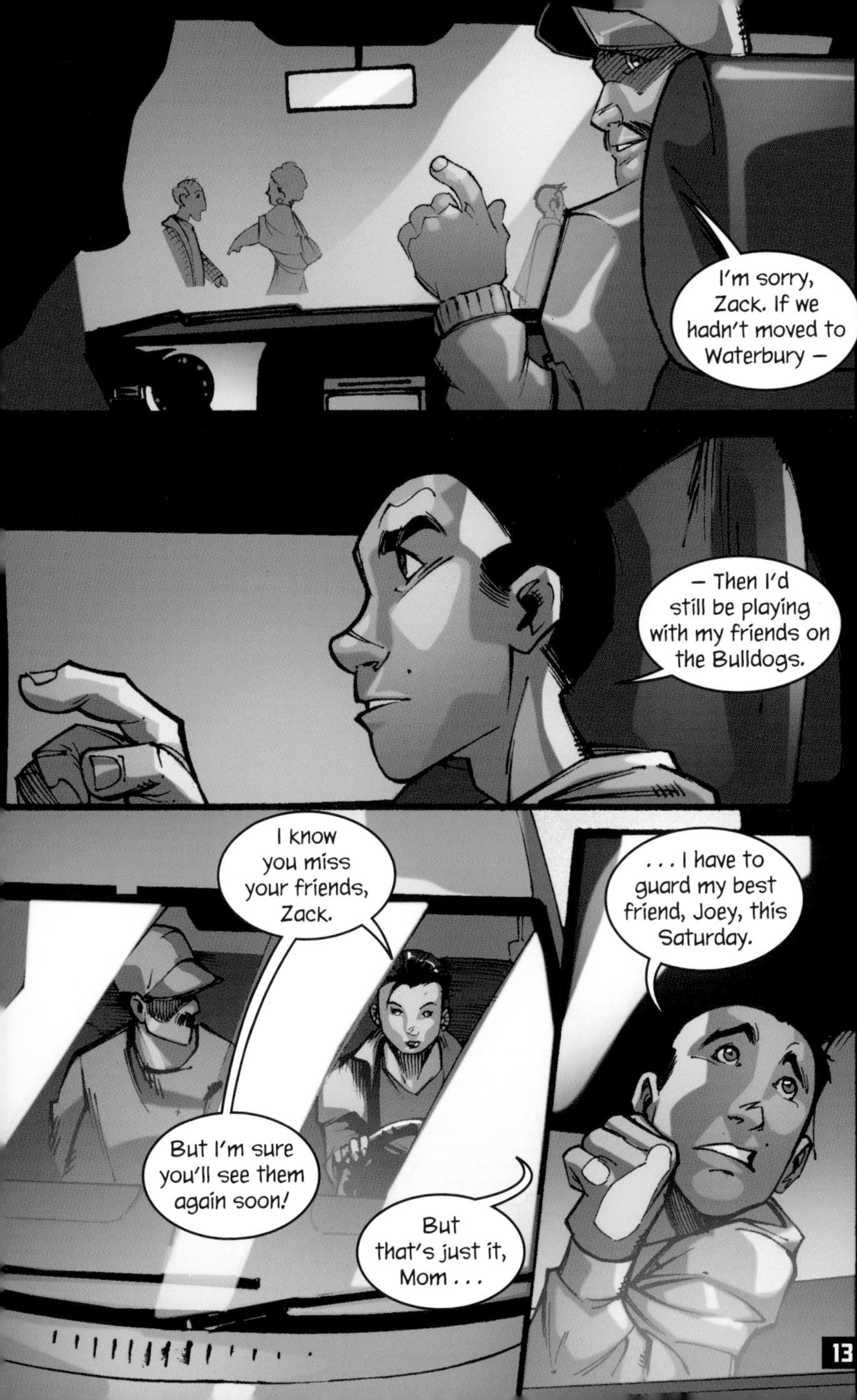
I'm sorry, Zack. If we hadn't moved to Waterbury –
– Then I'd still be playing with my friends on the Bulldogs.
I know you miss your friends, Zack.
But I'm sure you'll see them again soon!
But that's just it, Mom . . .
. . . I have to guard my best friend, Joey, this Saturday.

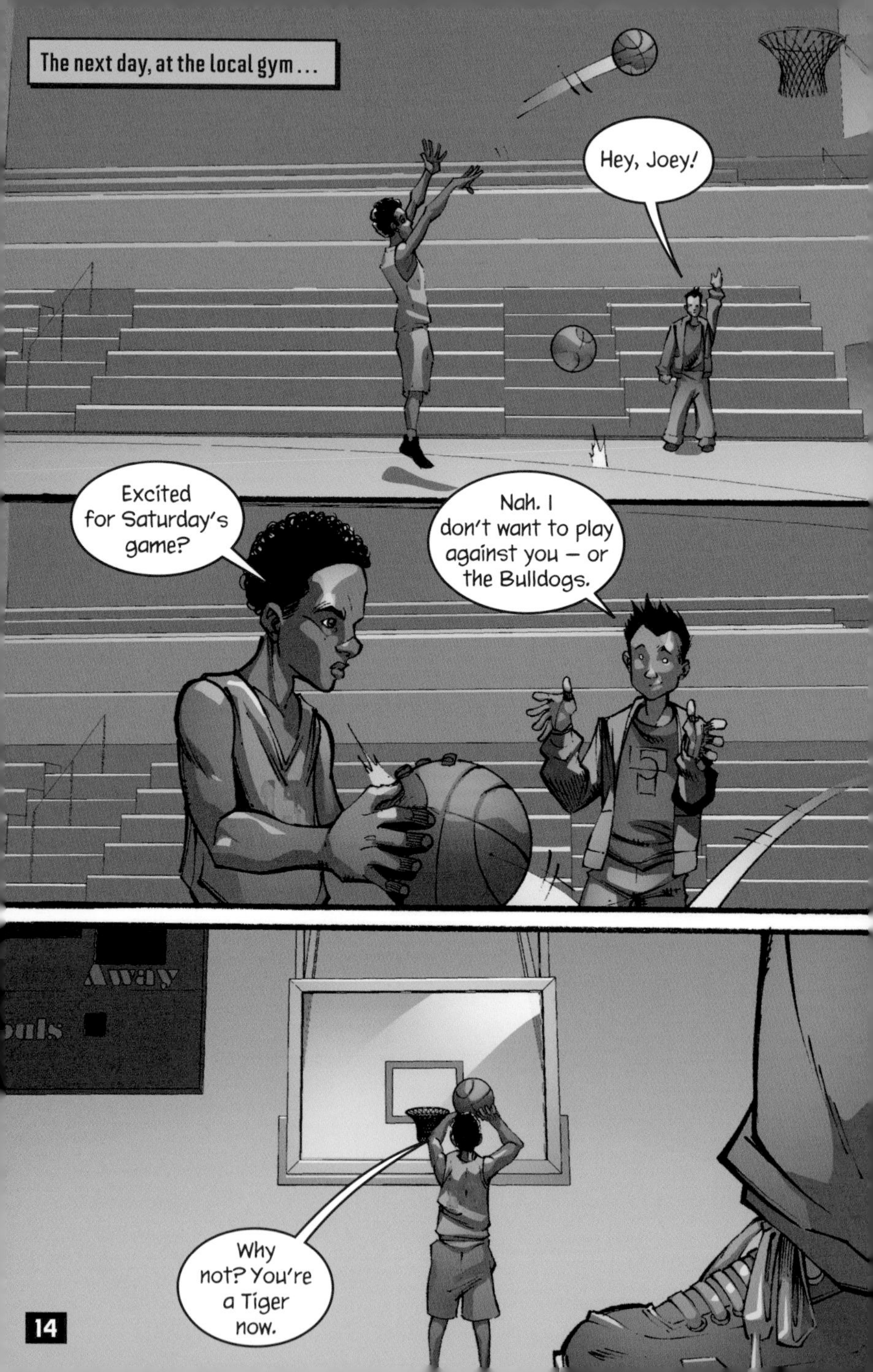

The next day, at the local gym . . .
Hey, Joey!
Excited for Saturday's game?
Nah. I don't want to play against you — or the Bulldogs.
Away
Why not? You're a Tiger now.

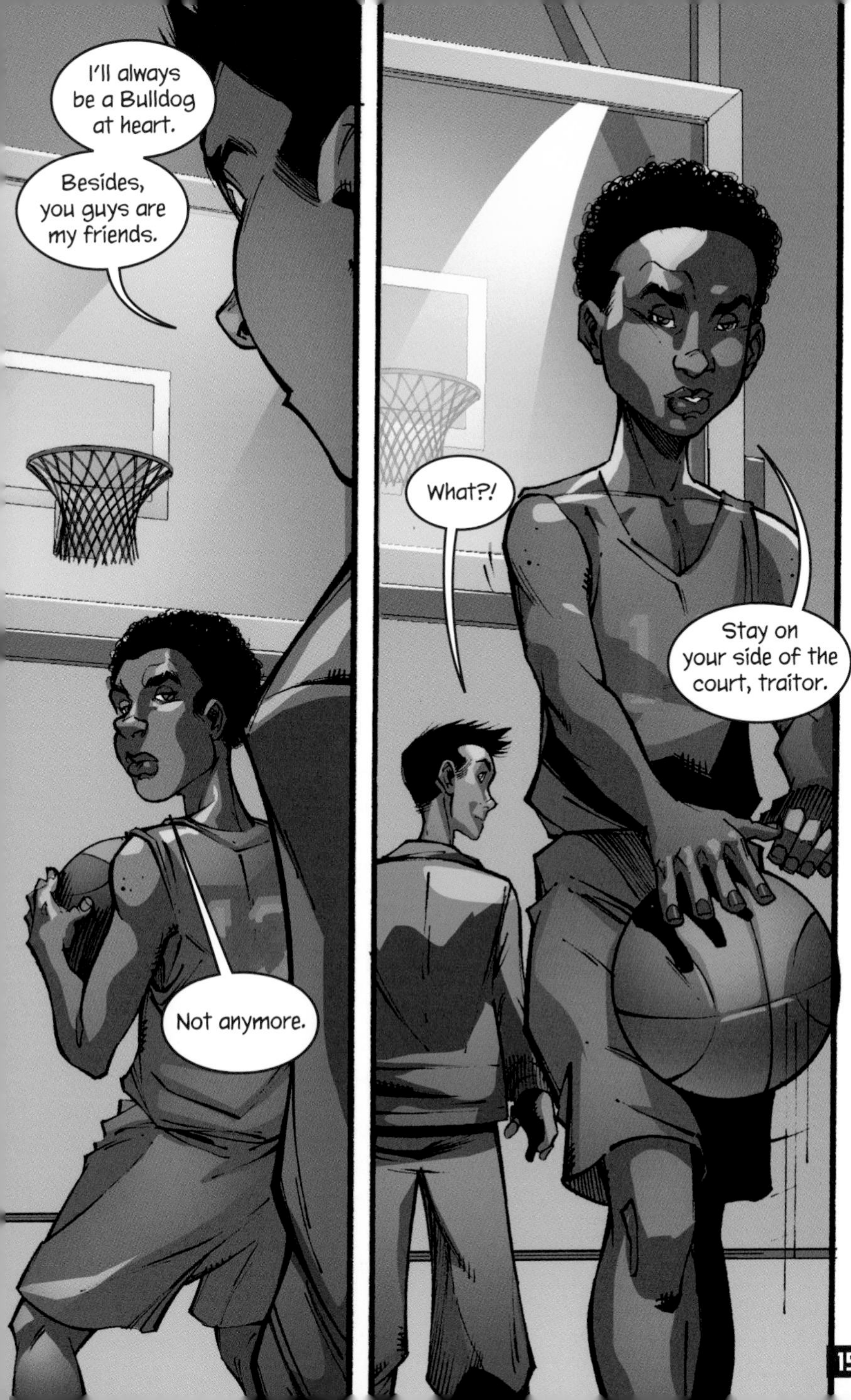

I'll always be a Bulldog at heart.
Besides, you guys are my friends.
Not anymore.
What?!
Stay on your side of the court, traitor.

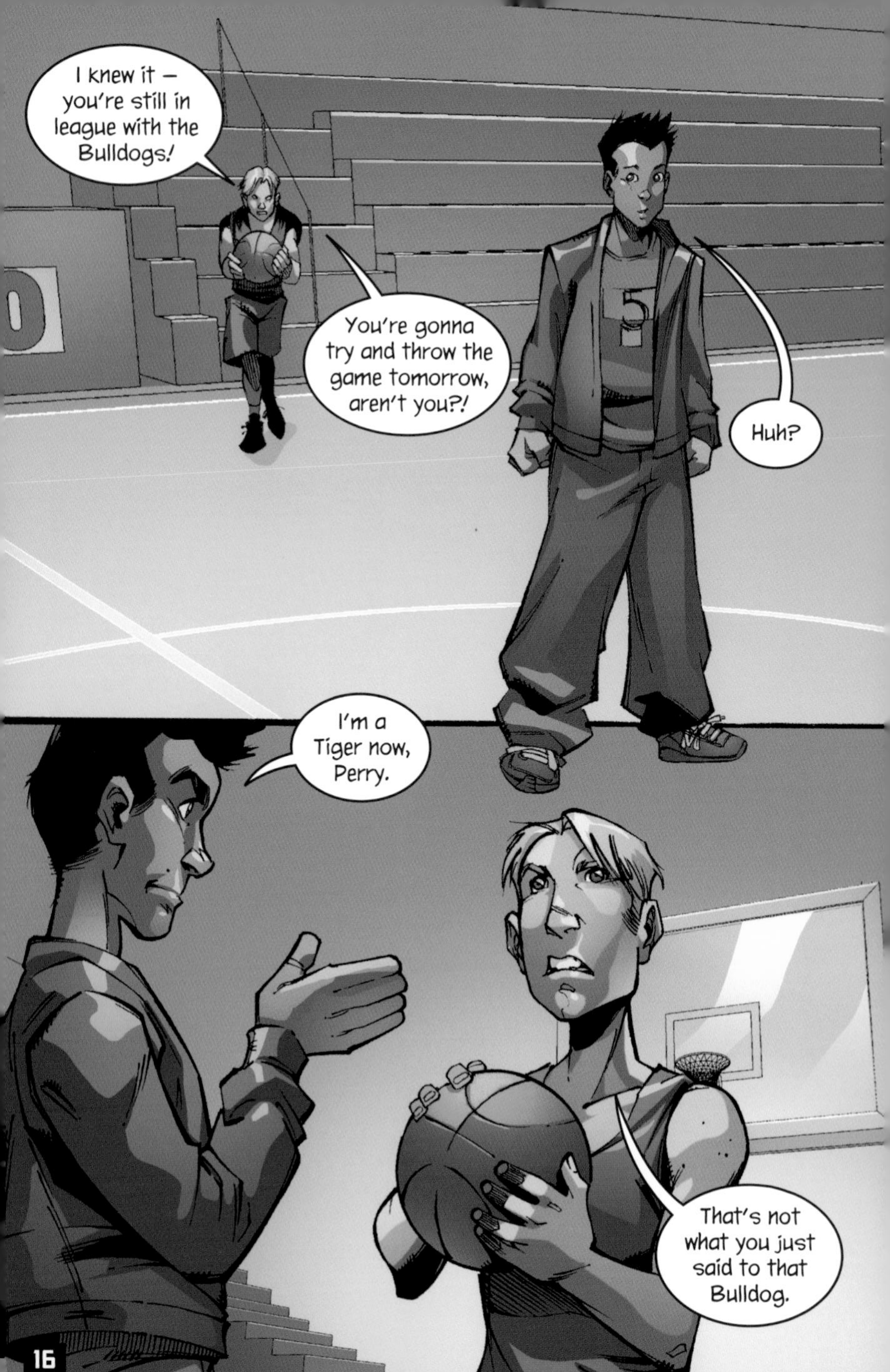
I knew it — you're still in league with the Bulldogs!
You're gonna try and throw the game tomorrow, aren't you?!
Huh?
I'm a Tiger now, Perry.
That's not what you just said to that Bulldog.

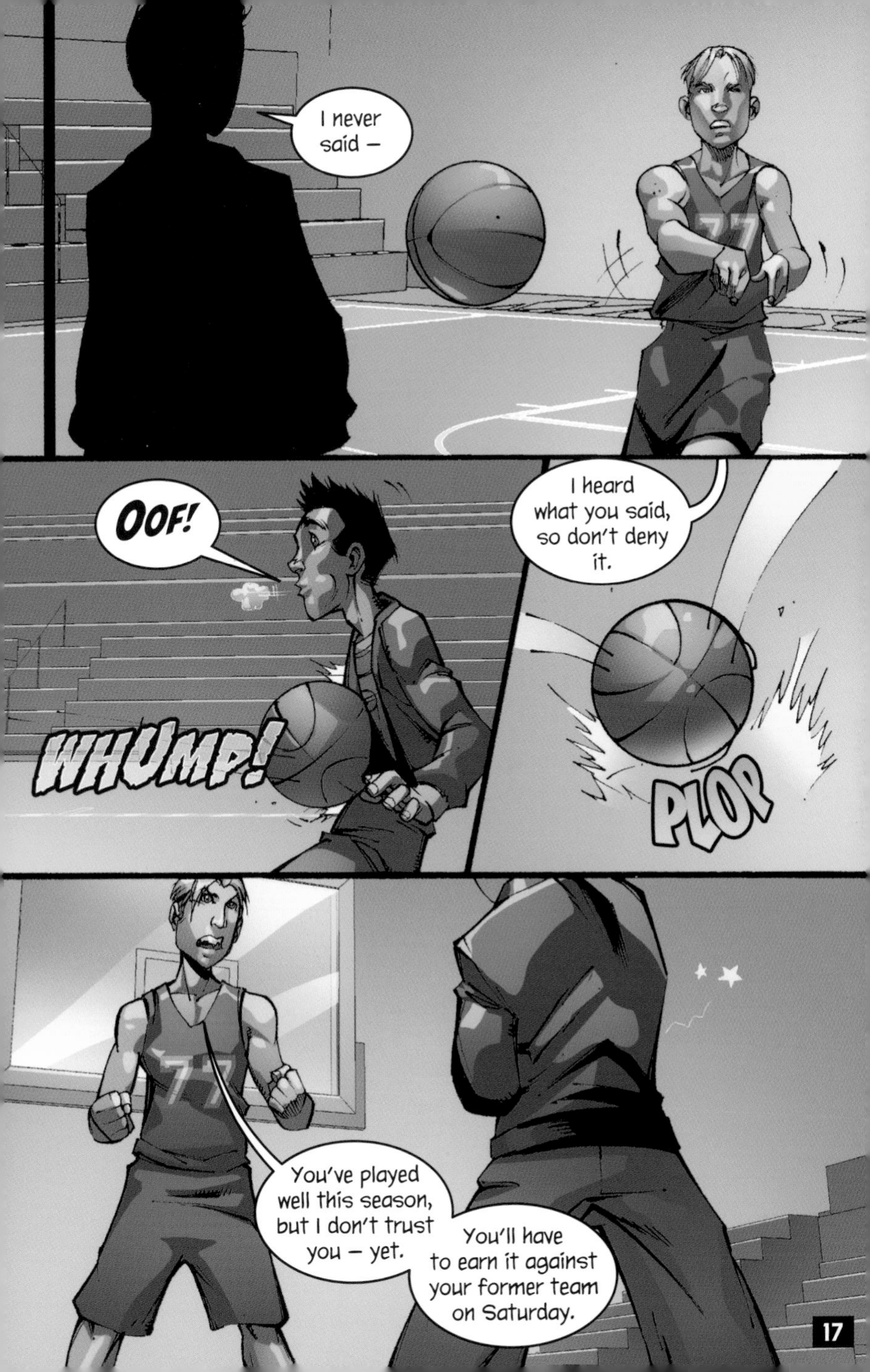
I never said —
OOF!
WHUMP!
I heard what you said, so don't deny it.
PLOP
You've played well this season, but I don't trust you — yet.
You'll have to earn it against your former team on Saturday.

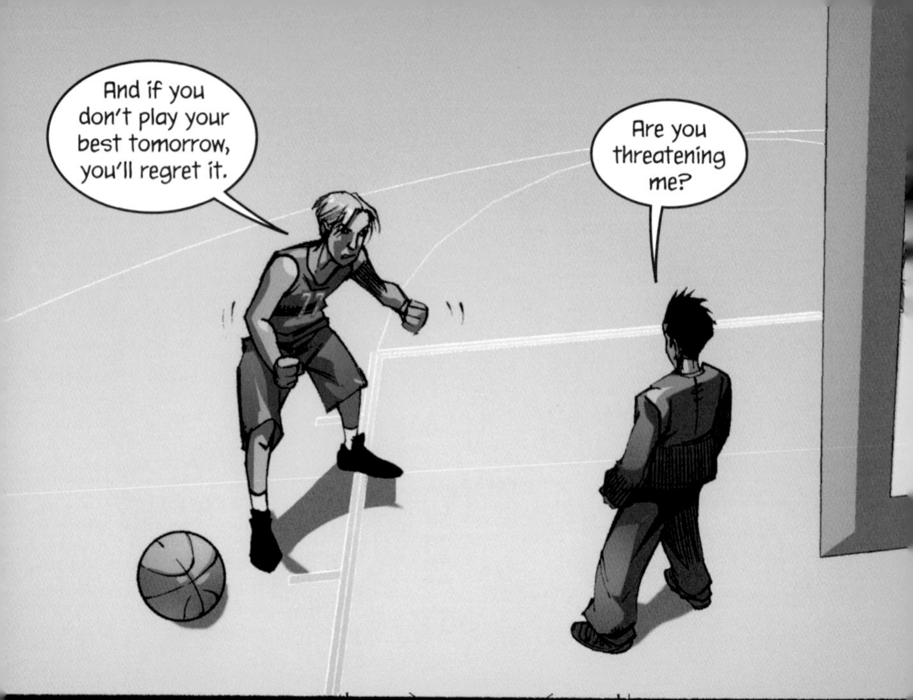
And if you don't play your best tomorrow, you'll regret it.
Are you threatening me?

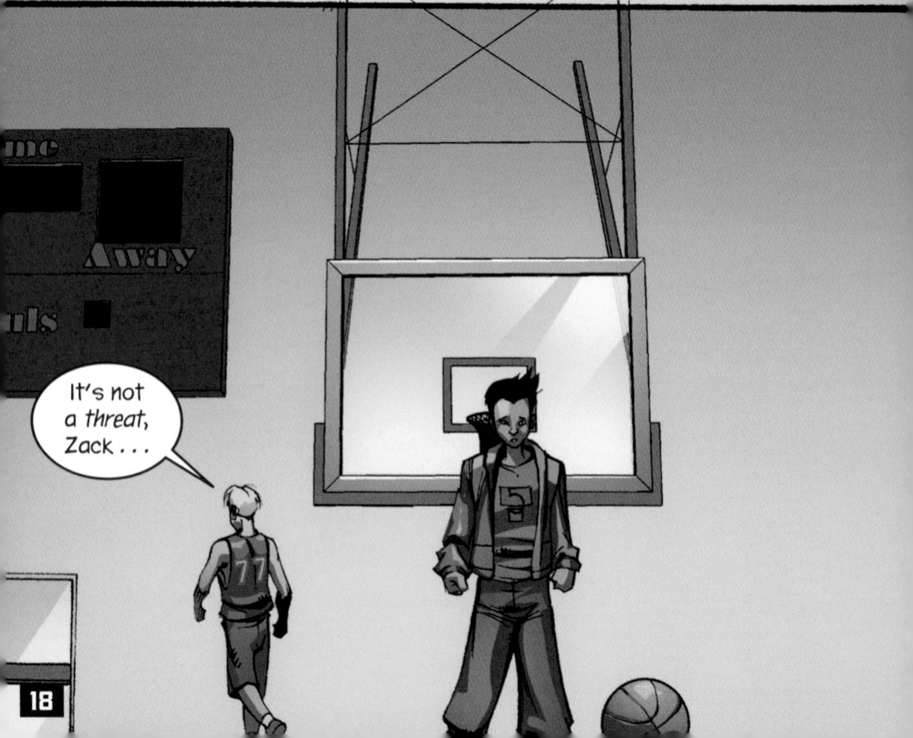
Away
It's not a *threat,* Zack . . .

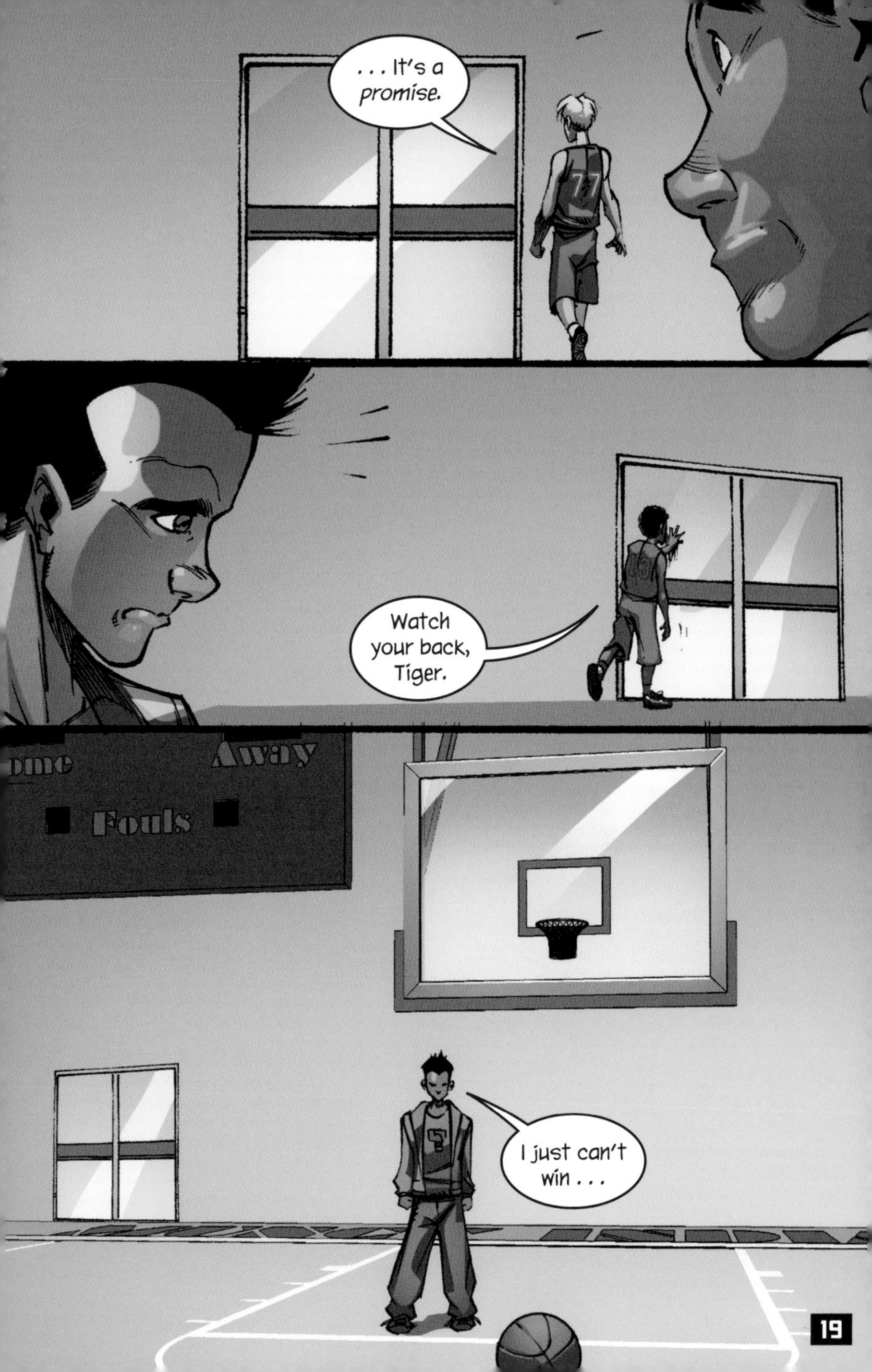
. . . It's a promise.
Watch your back, Tiger.
ome
Away
Fouls
I just can't win . . .

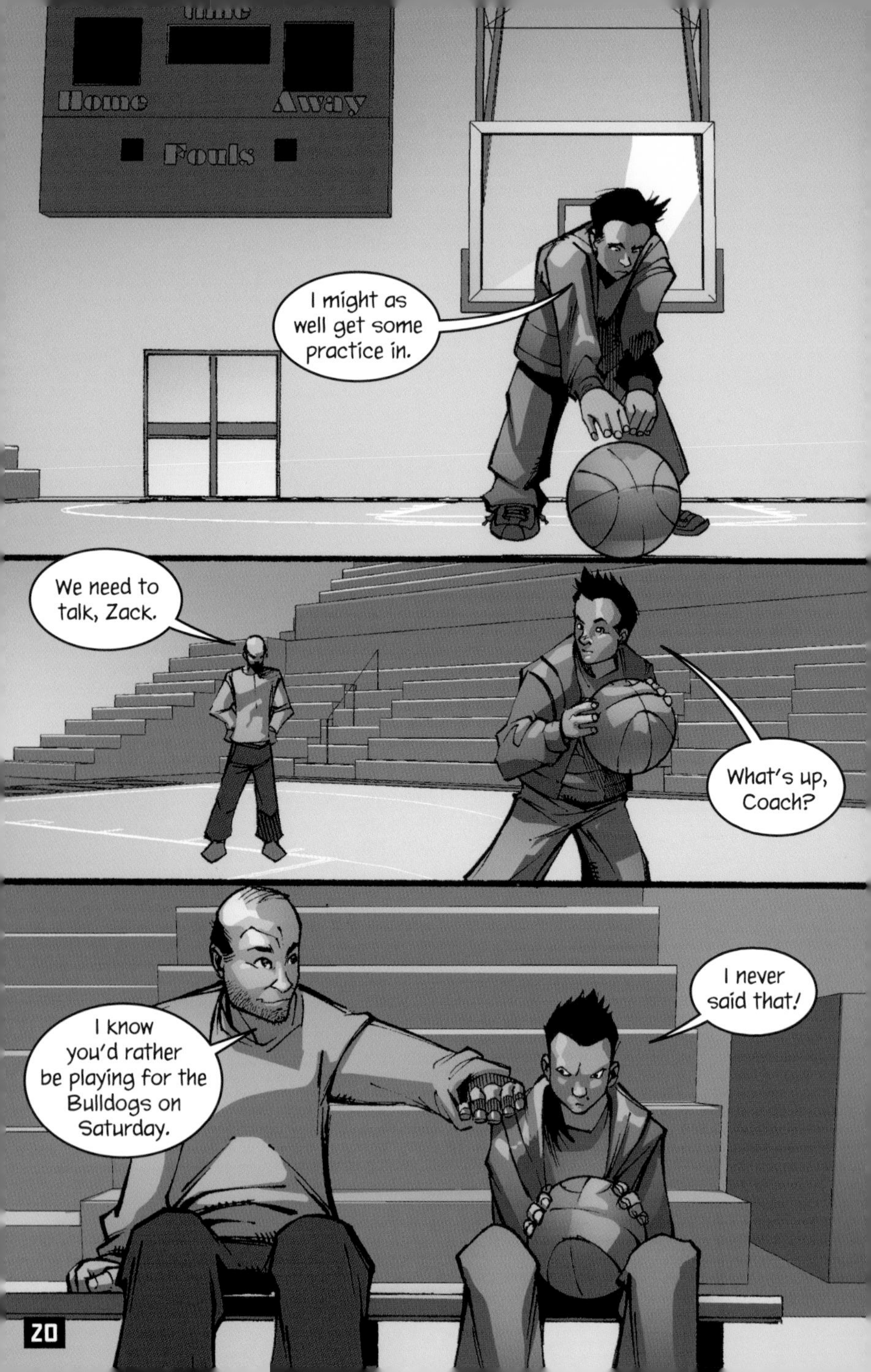
Home
Away
Fouls
I might as well get some practice in.
We need to talk, Zack.
What's up, Coach?
I know you'd rather be playing for the Bulldogs on Saturday.
I never said that!

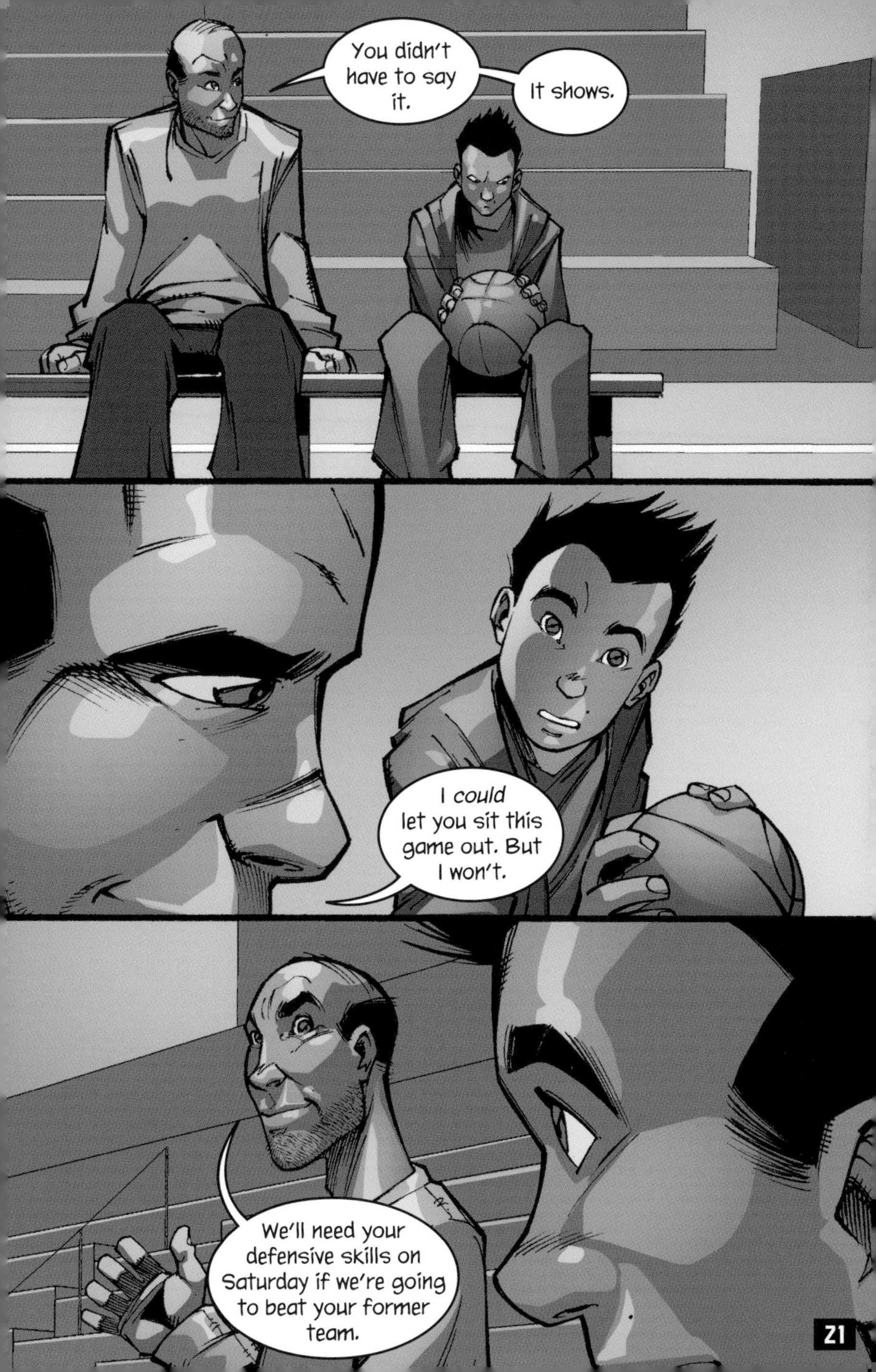
You didn't have to say it.
It shows.
I *could* let you sit this game out. But I won't.
We'll need your defensive skills on Saturday if we're going to beat your former team.

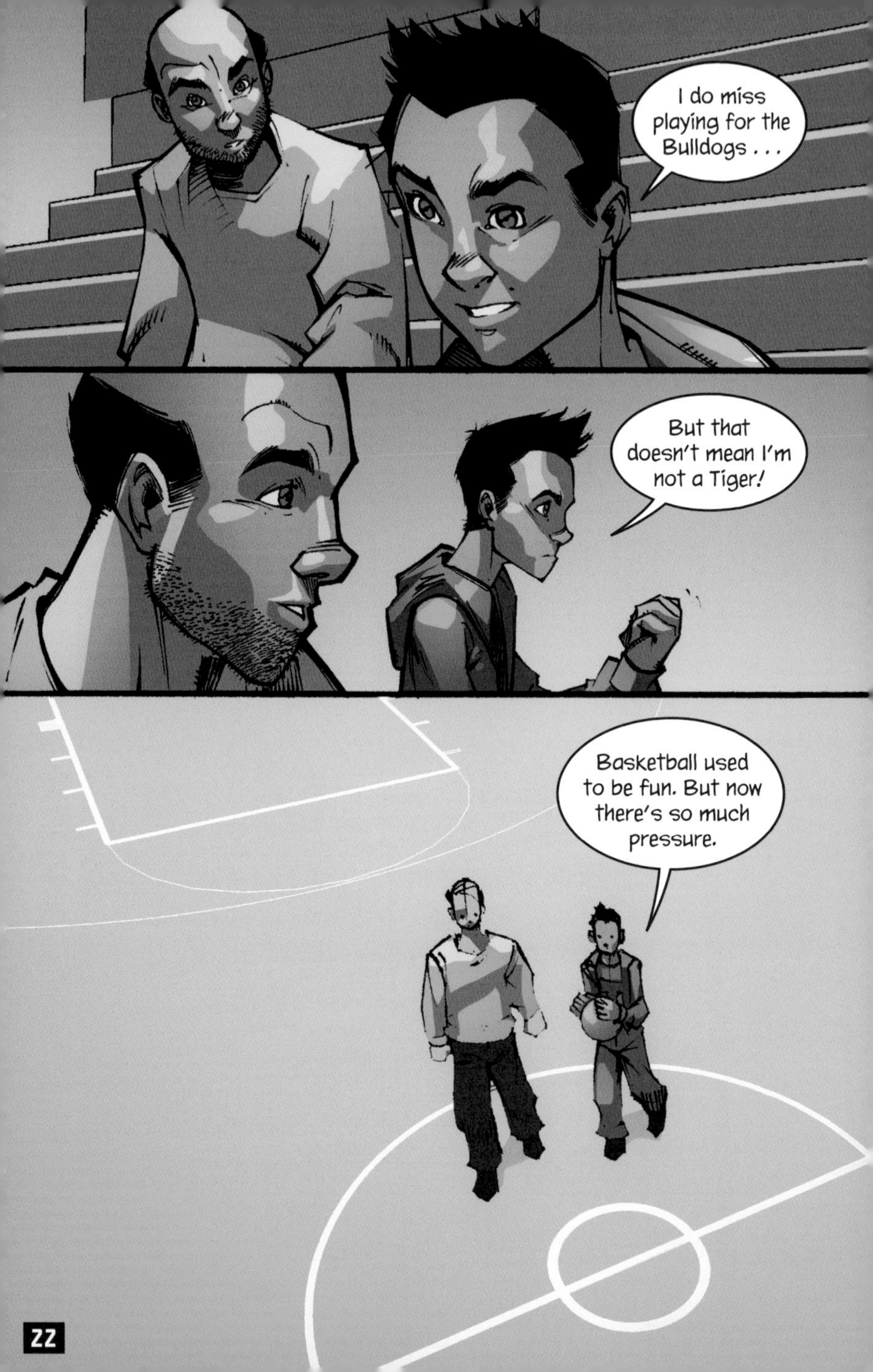
I do miss playing for the Bulldogs . . .
But that doesn't mean I'm not a Tiger!
Basketball used to be fun. But now there's so much pressure.

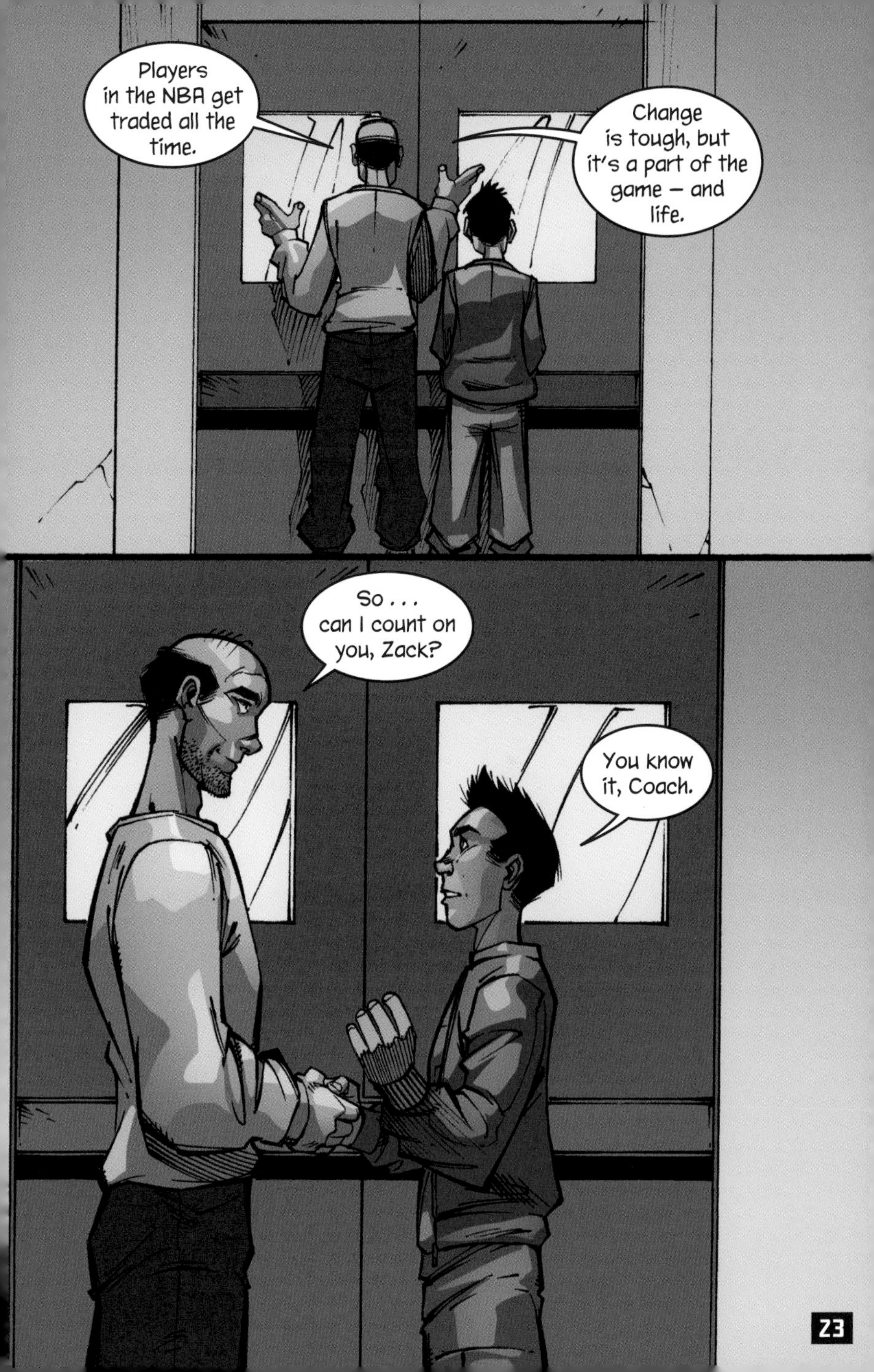
Players in the NBA get traded all the time.
Change is tough, but it's a part of the game — and life.
So . . . can I count on you, Zack?
You know it, Coach.

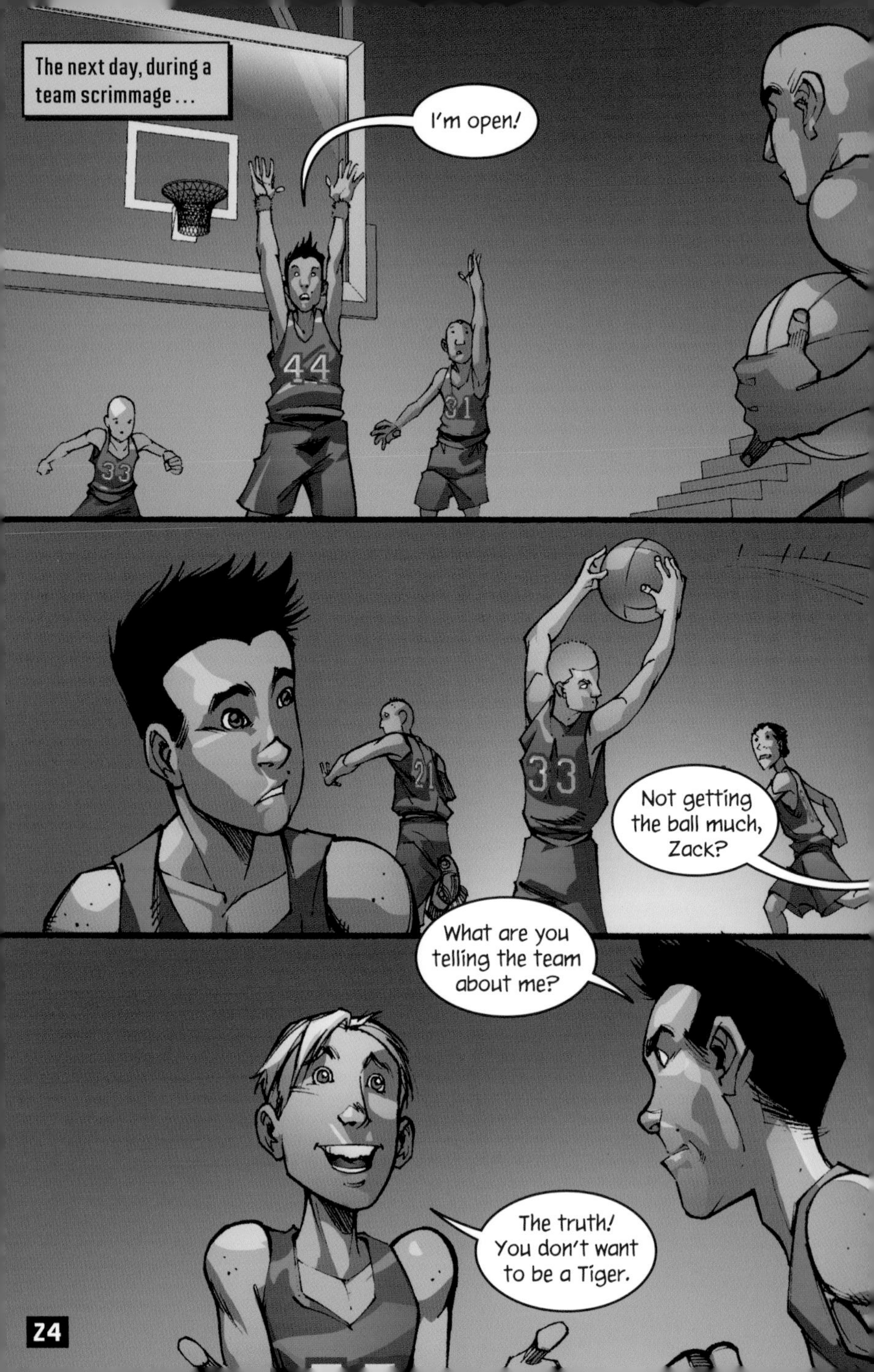
The next day, during a team scrimmage . . .
I'm open!
Not getting the ball much, Zack?
What are you telling the team about me?
The truth! You don't want to be a Tiger.

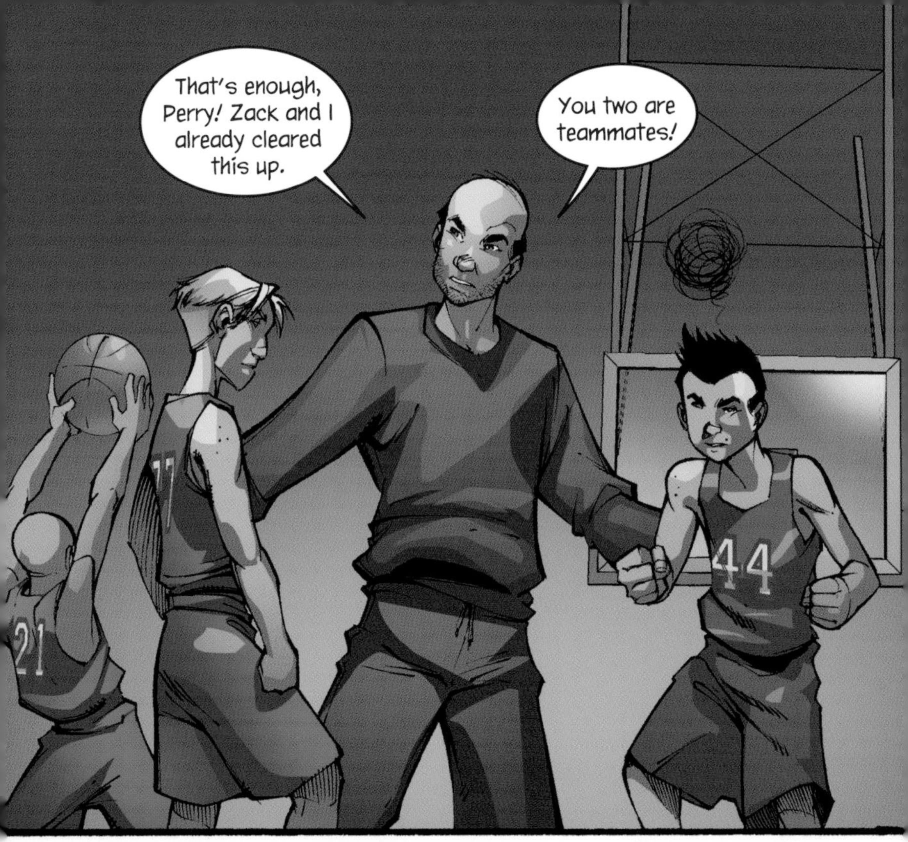
That's enough, Perry! Zack and I already cleared this up.
You two are teammates!

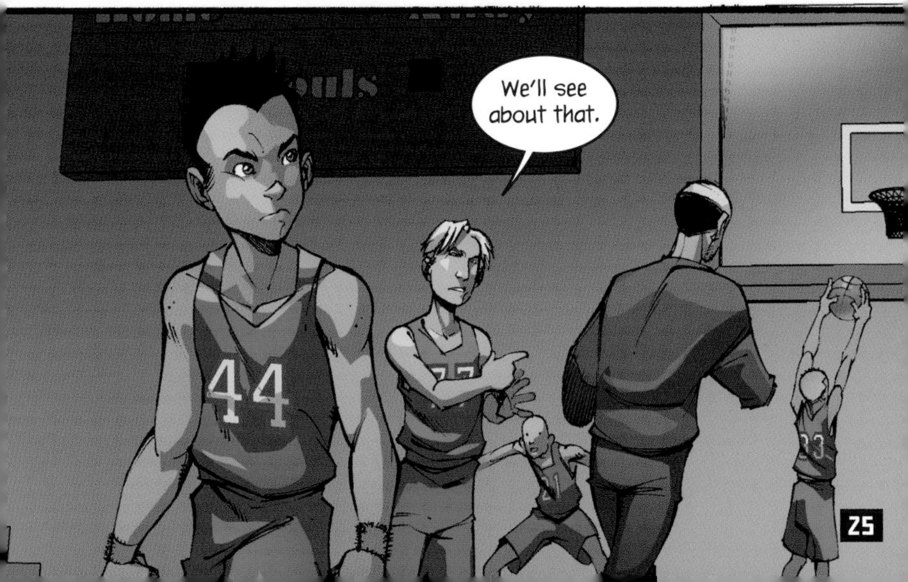
We'll see about that.

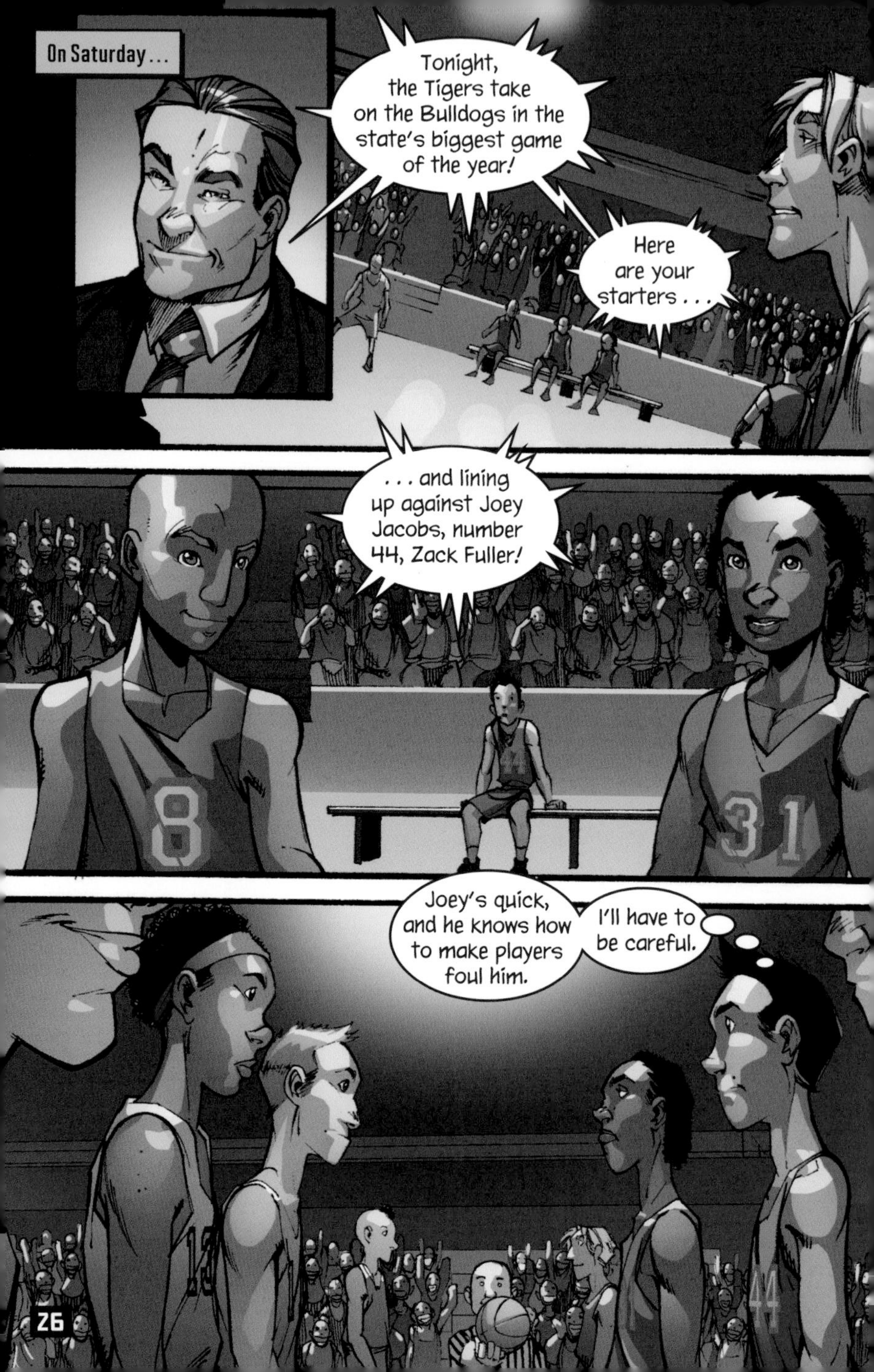

On Saturday . . .
Tonight, the Tigers take on the Bulldogs in the state's biggest game of the year!
Here are your starters . . .
. . . and lining up against Joey Jacobs, number 44, Zack Fuller!
Joey's quick, and he knows how to make players foul him.
I'll have to be careful.

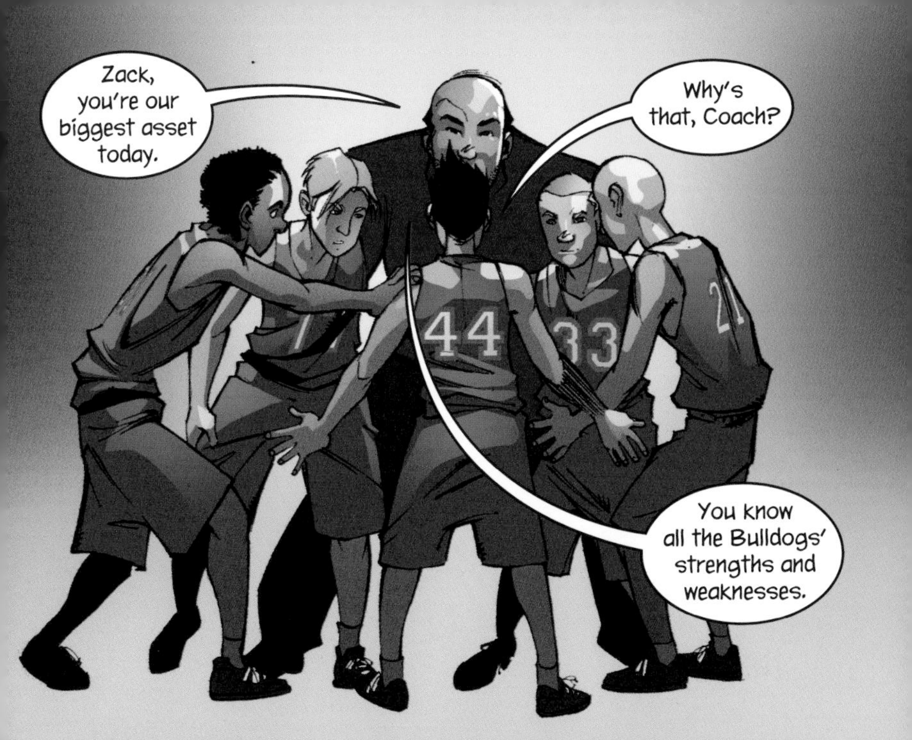
Zack, you're our biggest asset today.
Why's that, Coach?
You know all the Bulldogs' strengths and weaknesses.

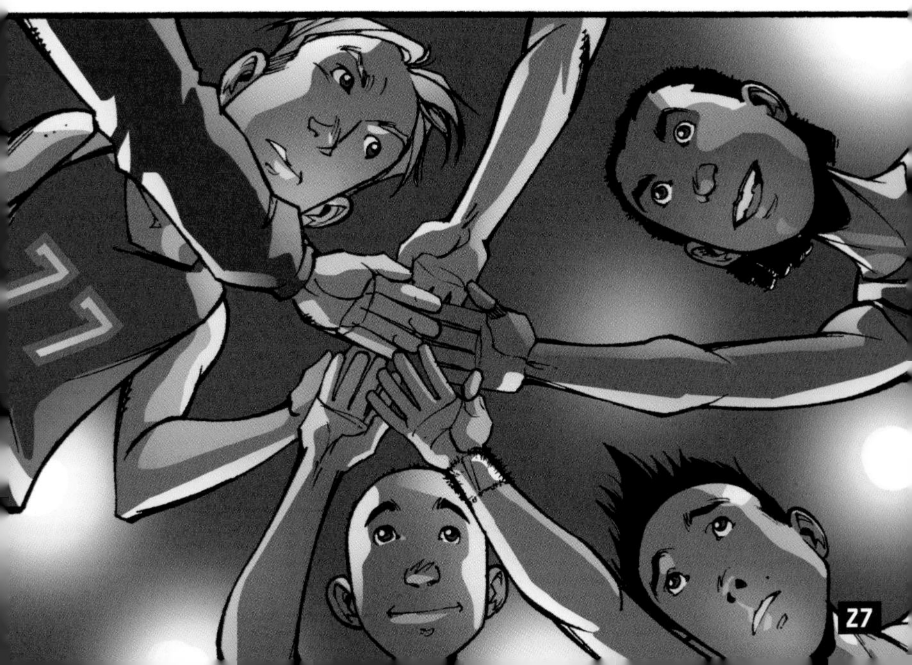

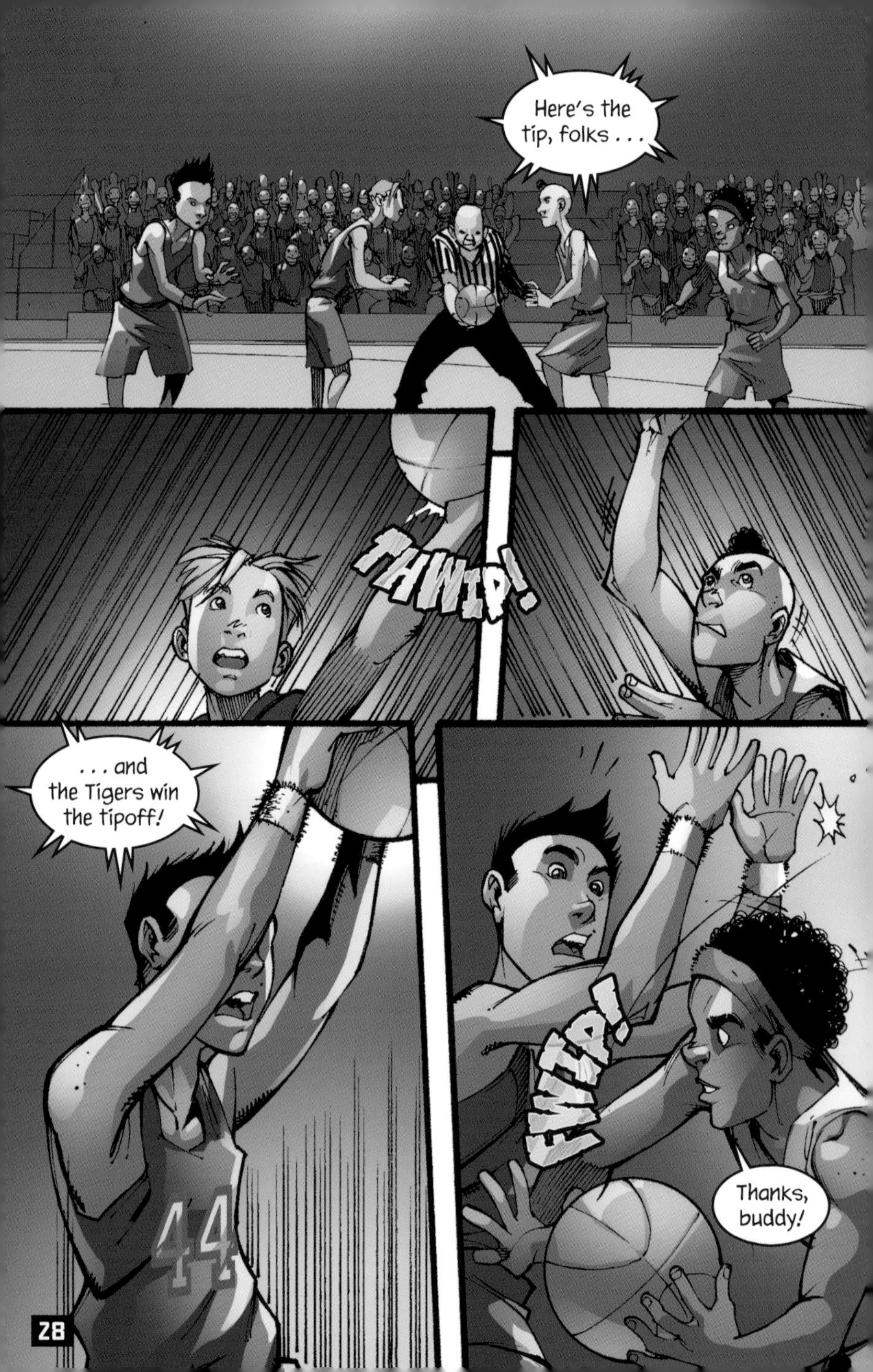
Here's the tip, folks . . .
THWIP!
. . . and the Tigers win the tipoff!
FWIP!
Thanks, buddy!

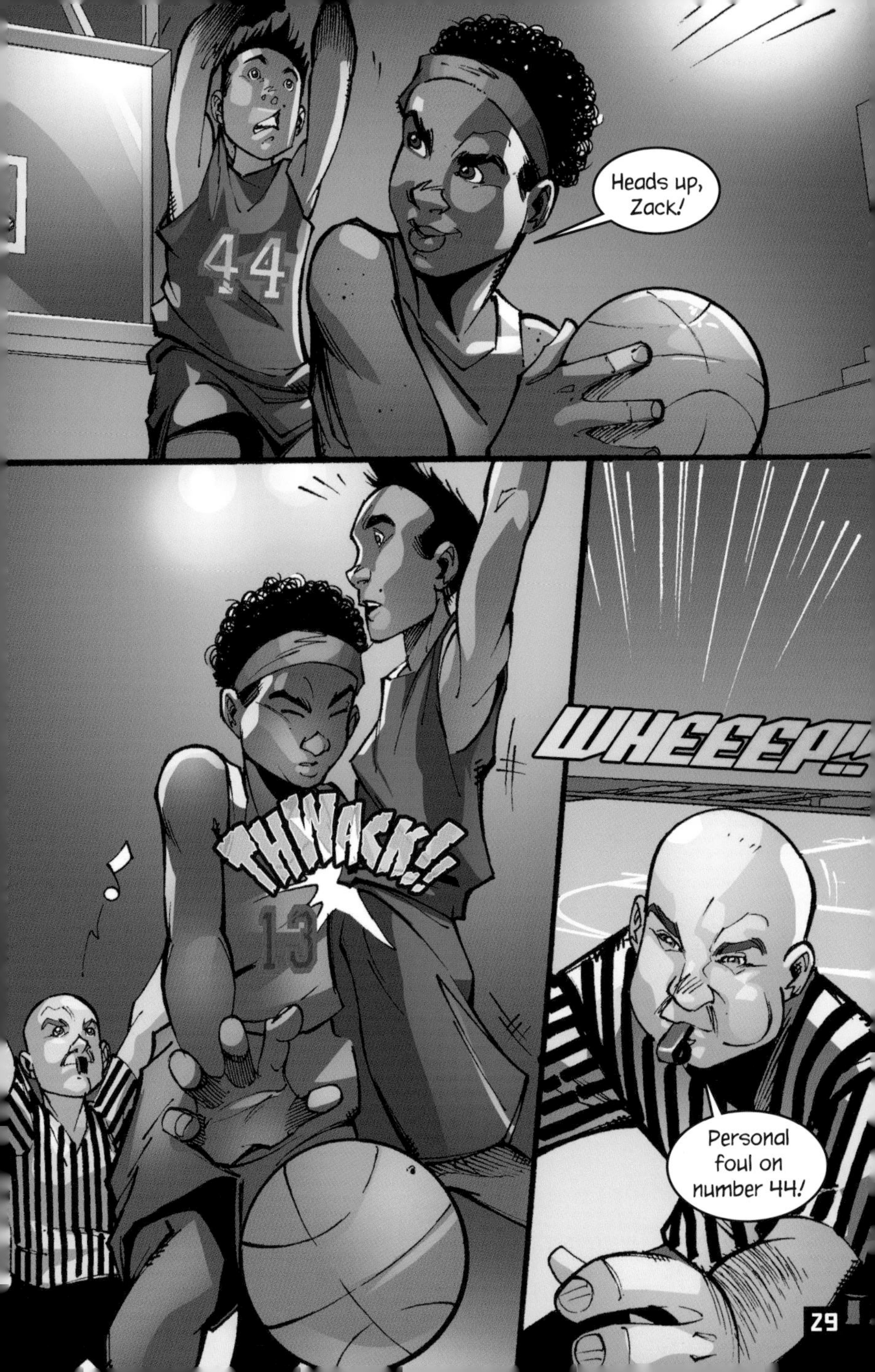
Heads up, Zack!
THWACK!!
WHEEEP!!
Personal foul on number 44!

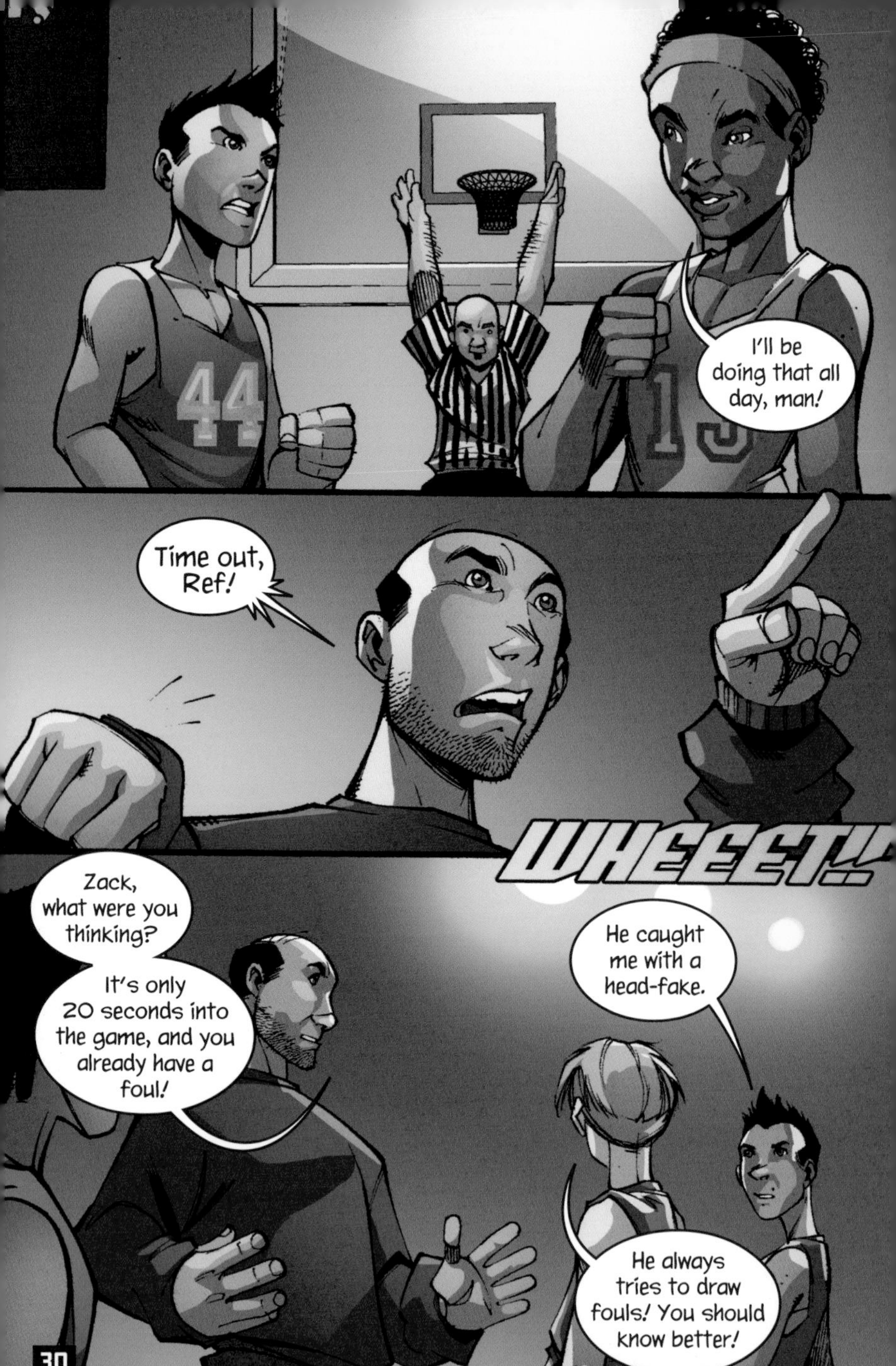
I'll be doing that all day, man!
Time out, Ref!
WHEEET!!
Zack, what were you thinking?
It's only 20 seconds into the game, and you already have a foul!
He caught me with a head-fake.
He always tries to draw fouls! You should know better!

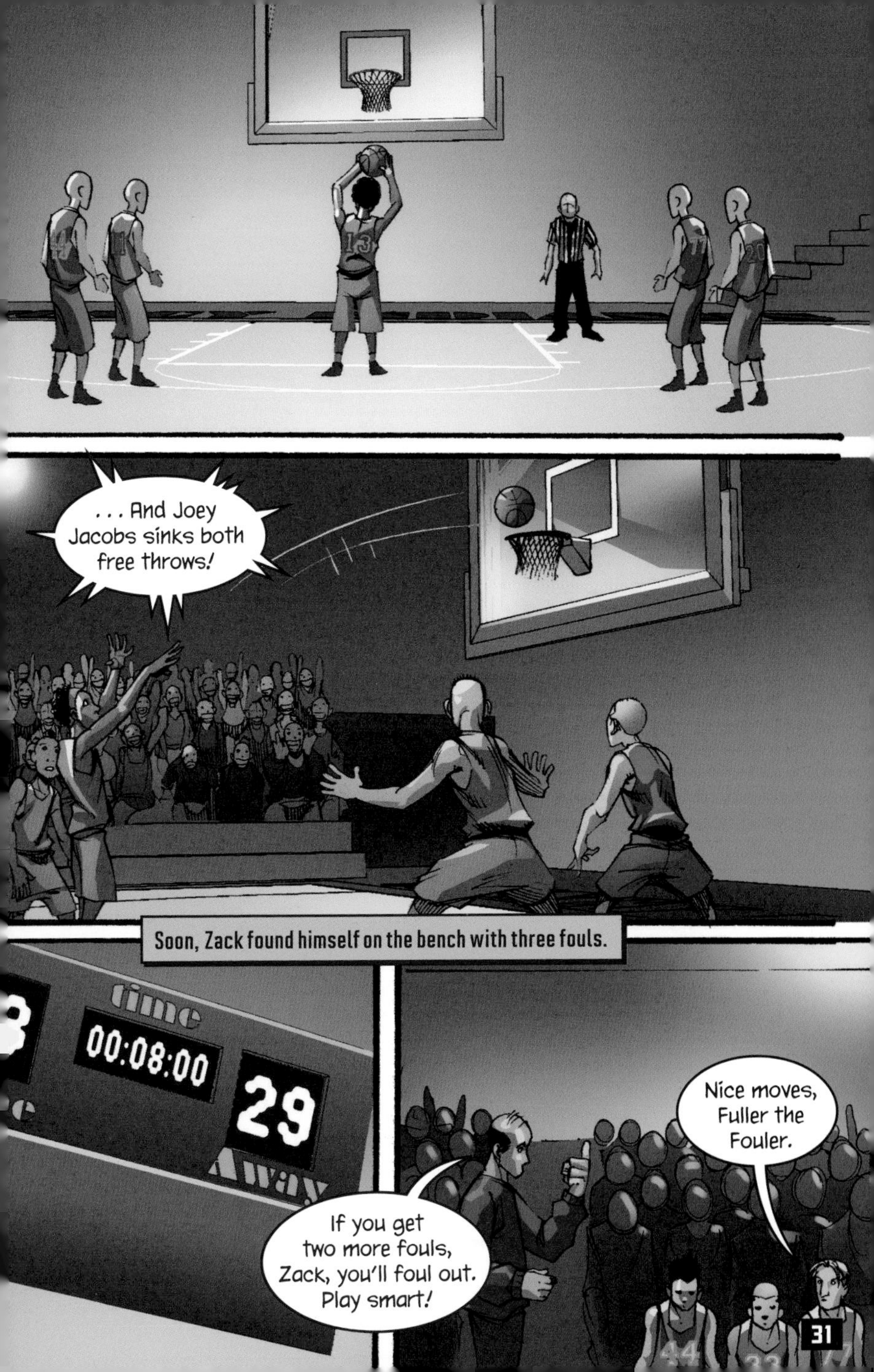
. . . And Joey Jacobs sinks both free throws!
Soon, Zack found himself on the bench with three fouls.
time
00:08:00
29
Away
If you get two more fouls, Zack, you'll foul out. Play smart!
Nice moves, Fuller the Fouler.

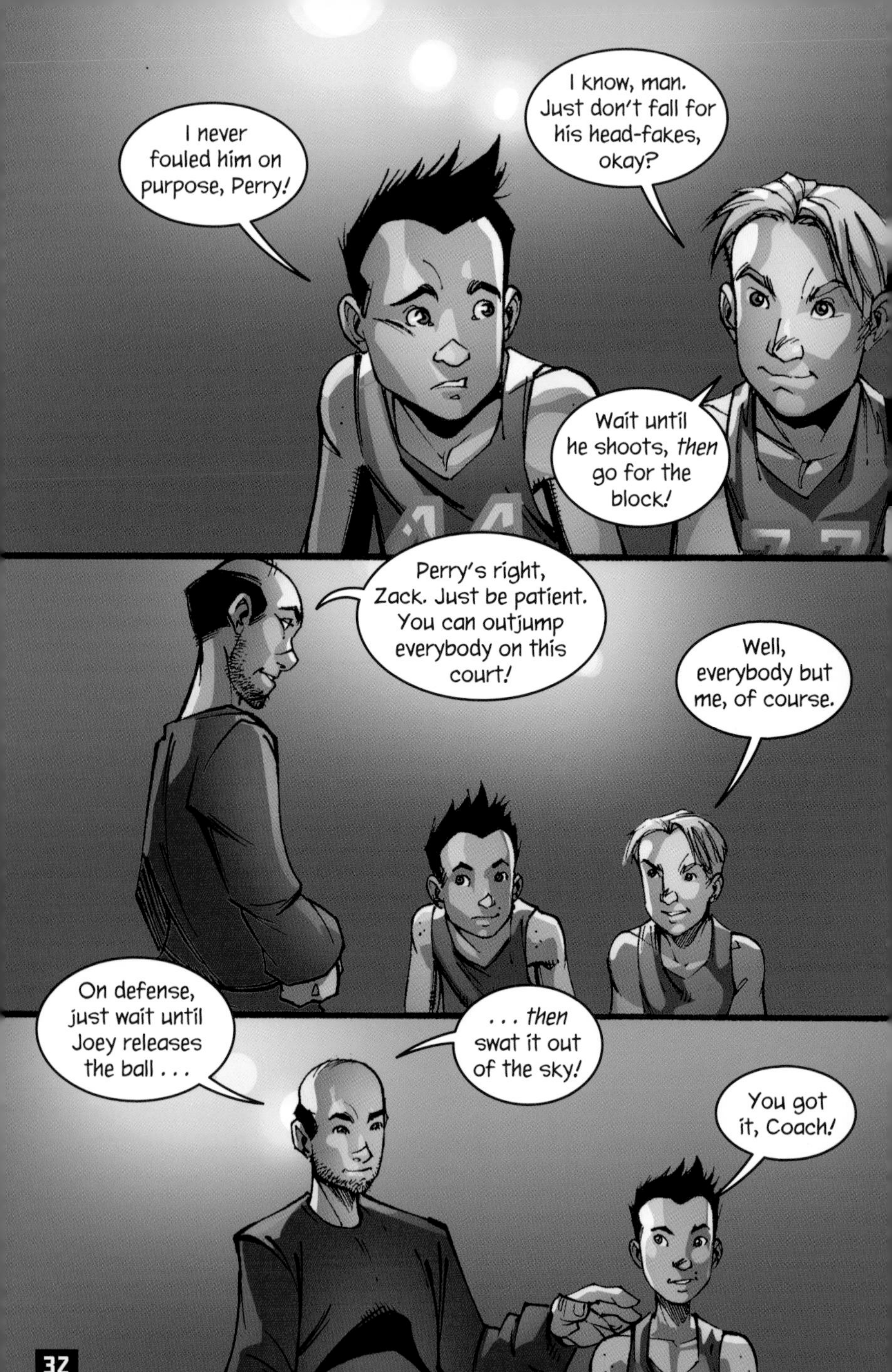

I never fouled him on purpose, Perry!
I know, man. Just don't fall for his head-fakes, okay?
Wait until he shoots, *then* go for the block!
Perry's right, Zack. Just be patient. You can outjump everybody on this court!
Well, everybody but me, of course.
On defense, just wait until Joey releases the ball . . .
. . . *then* swat it out of the sky!
You got it, Coach!

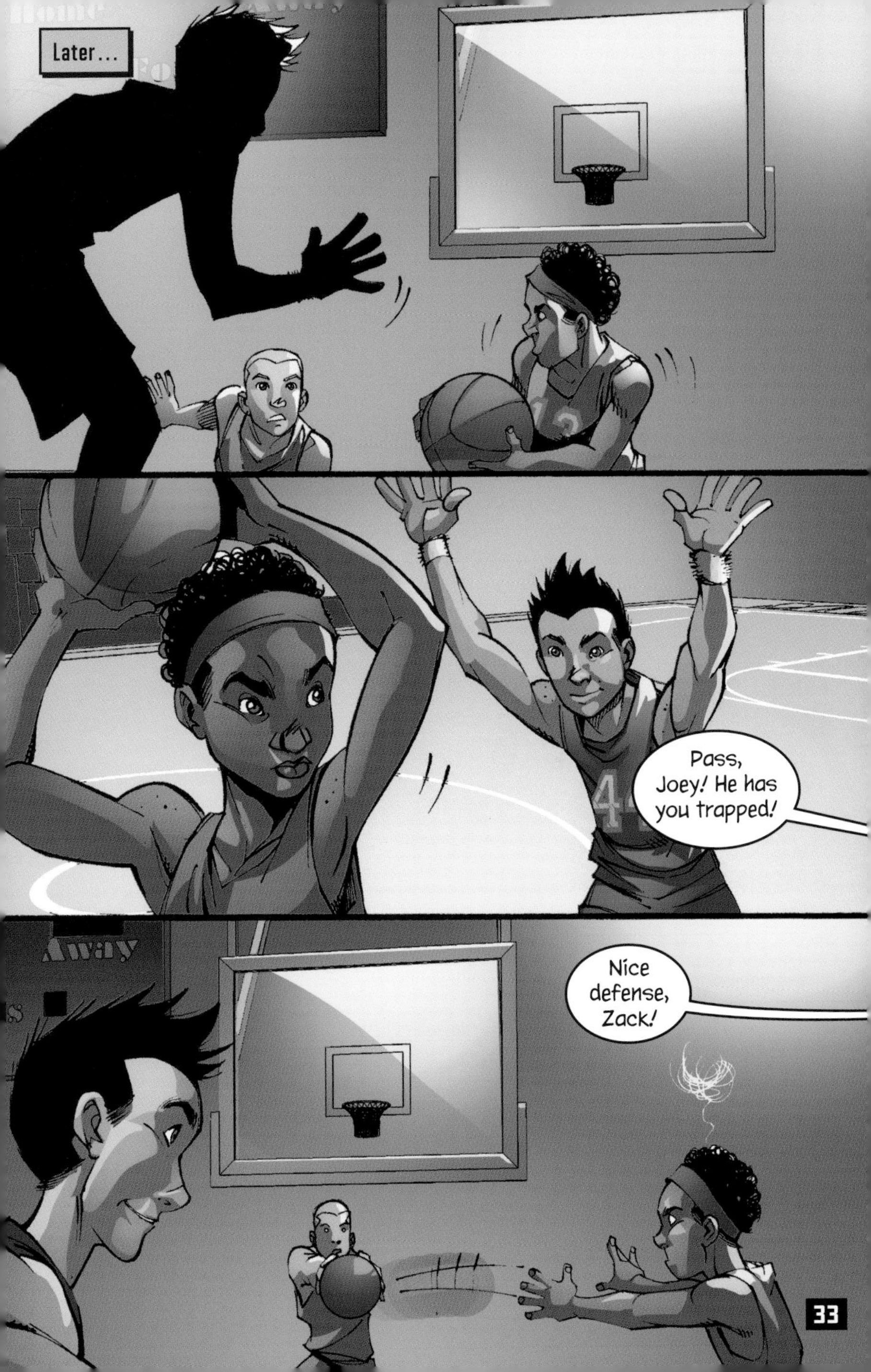
Later...
Pass, Joey! He has you trapped!
Nice defense, Zack!

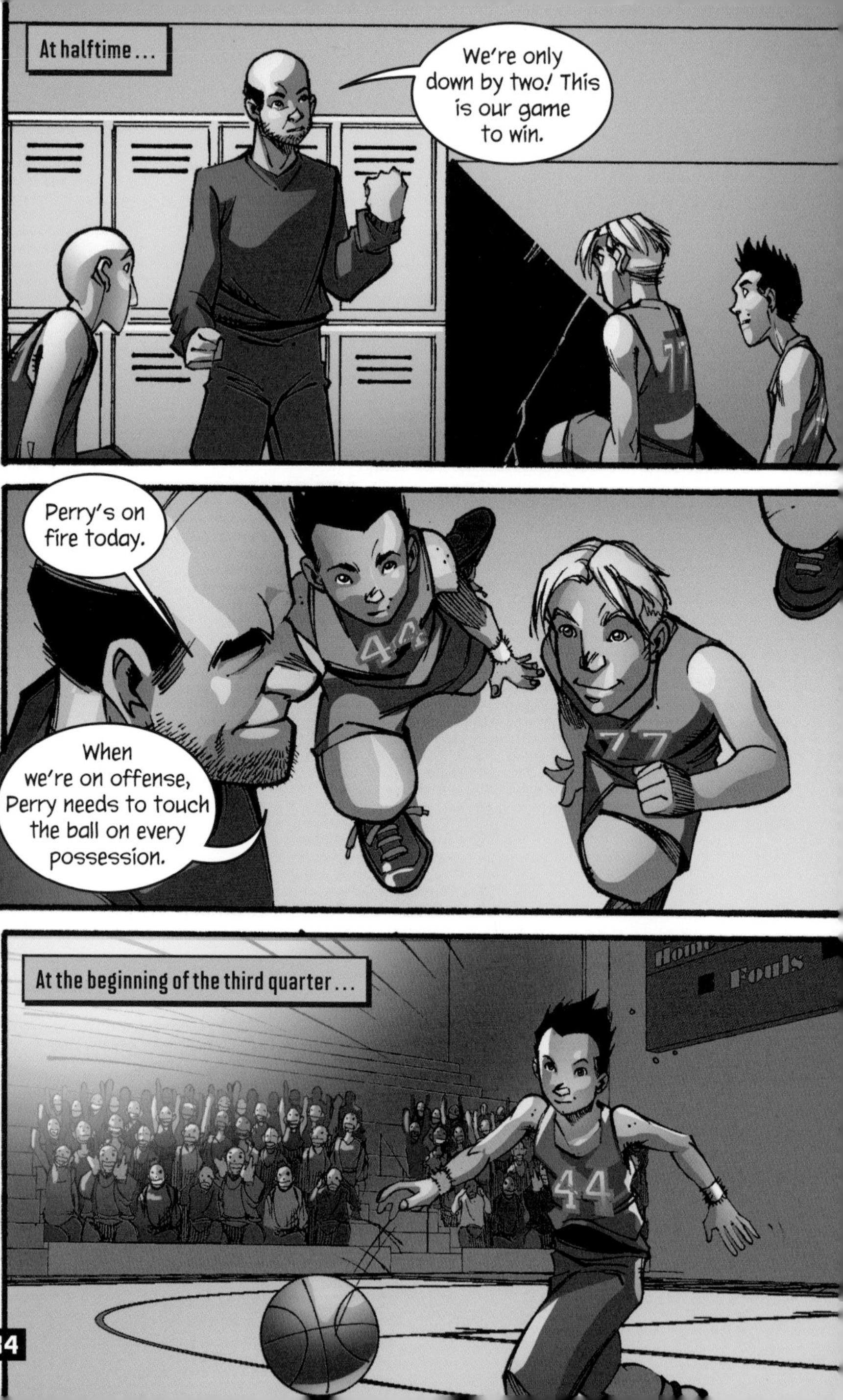

At halftime...
We're only down by two! This is our game to win.
Perry's on fire today.
When we're on offense, Perry needs to touch the ball on every possession.
At the beginning of the third quarter...

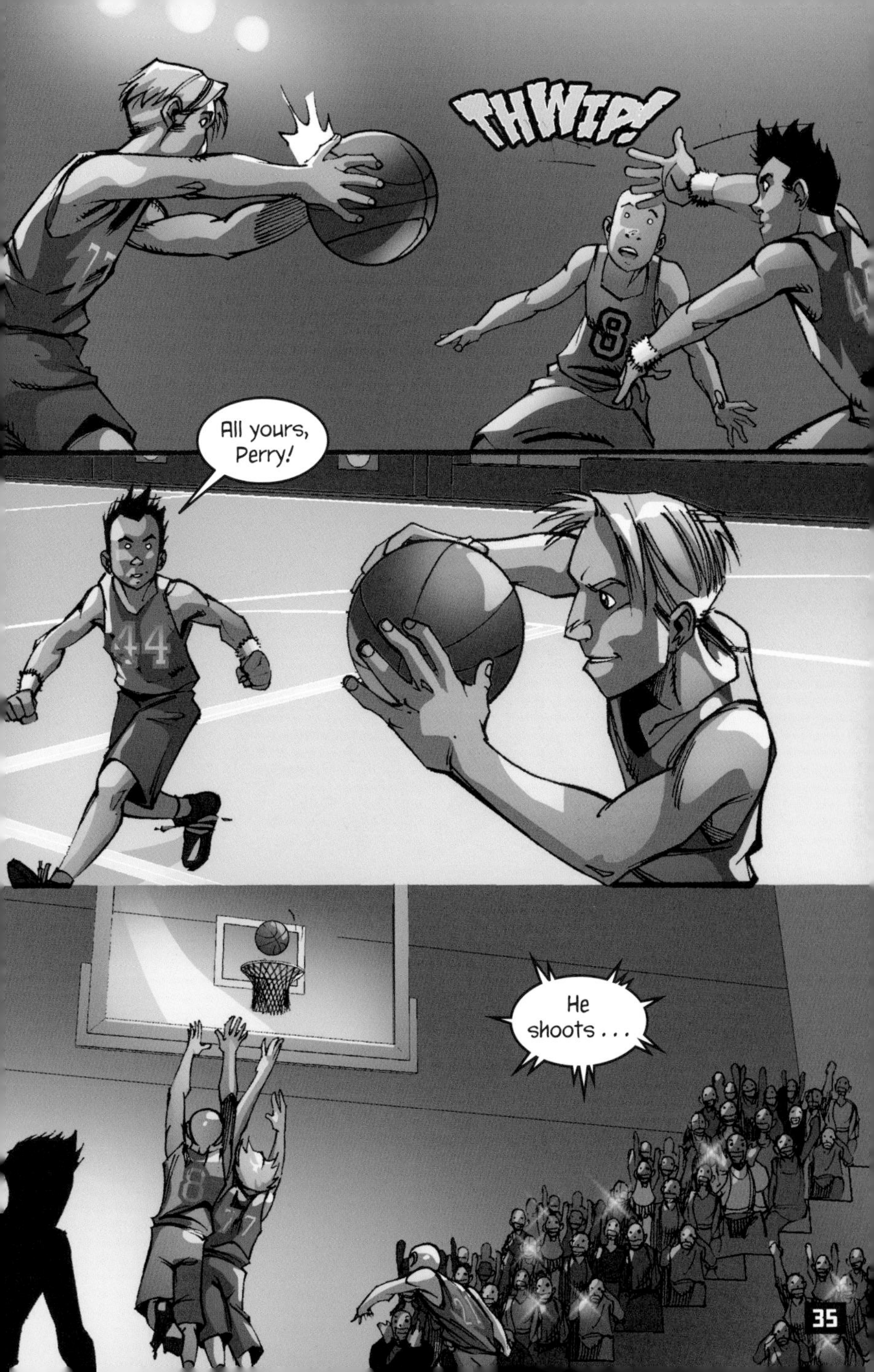
THWIP!
All yours, Perry!
He shoots . . .

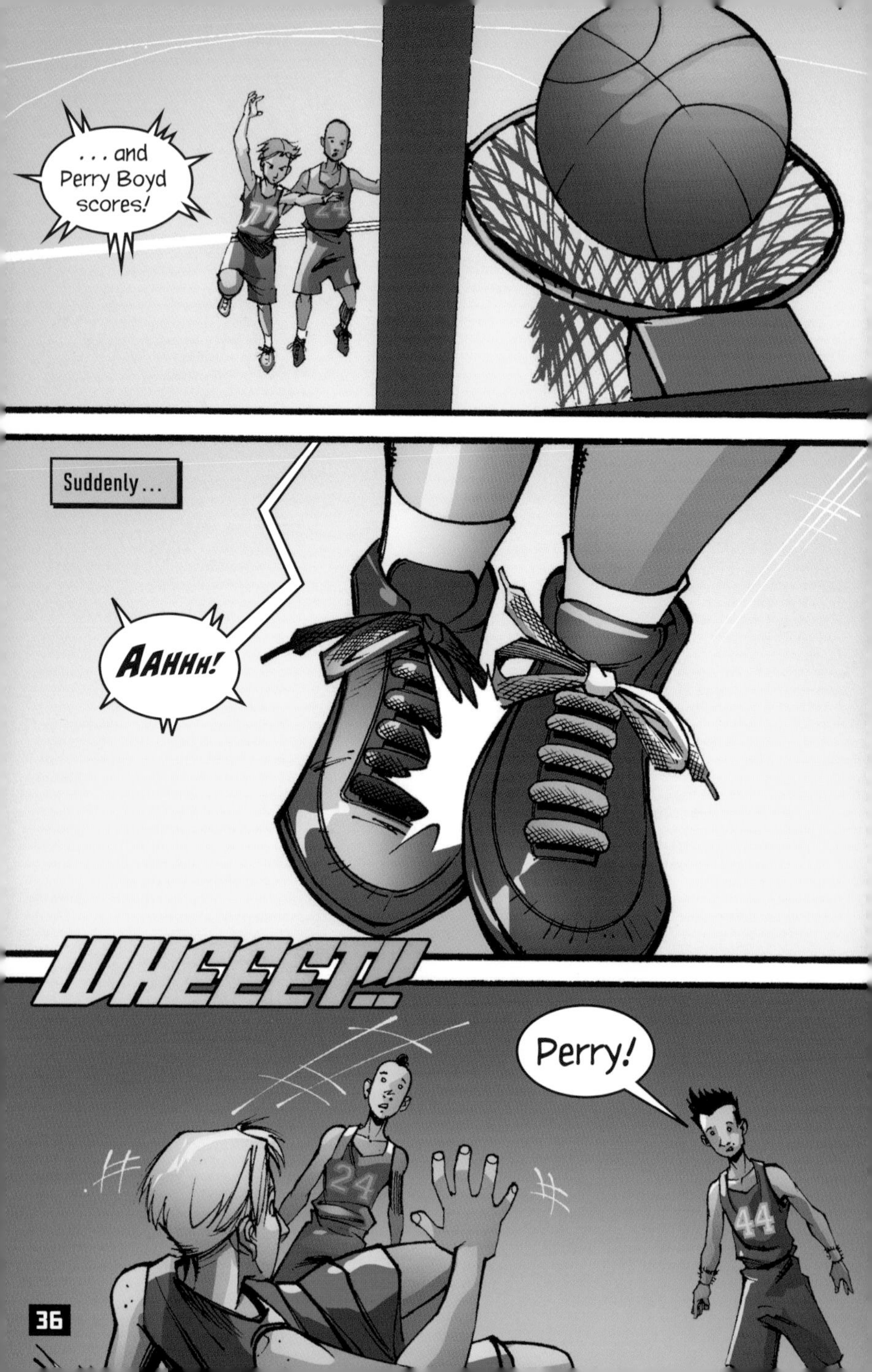
. . . and Perry Boyd scores!
Suddenly . . .
AAHHH!
WHEEET!!
Perry!

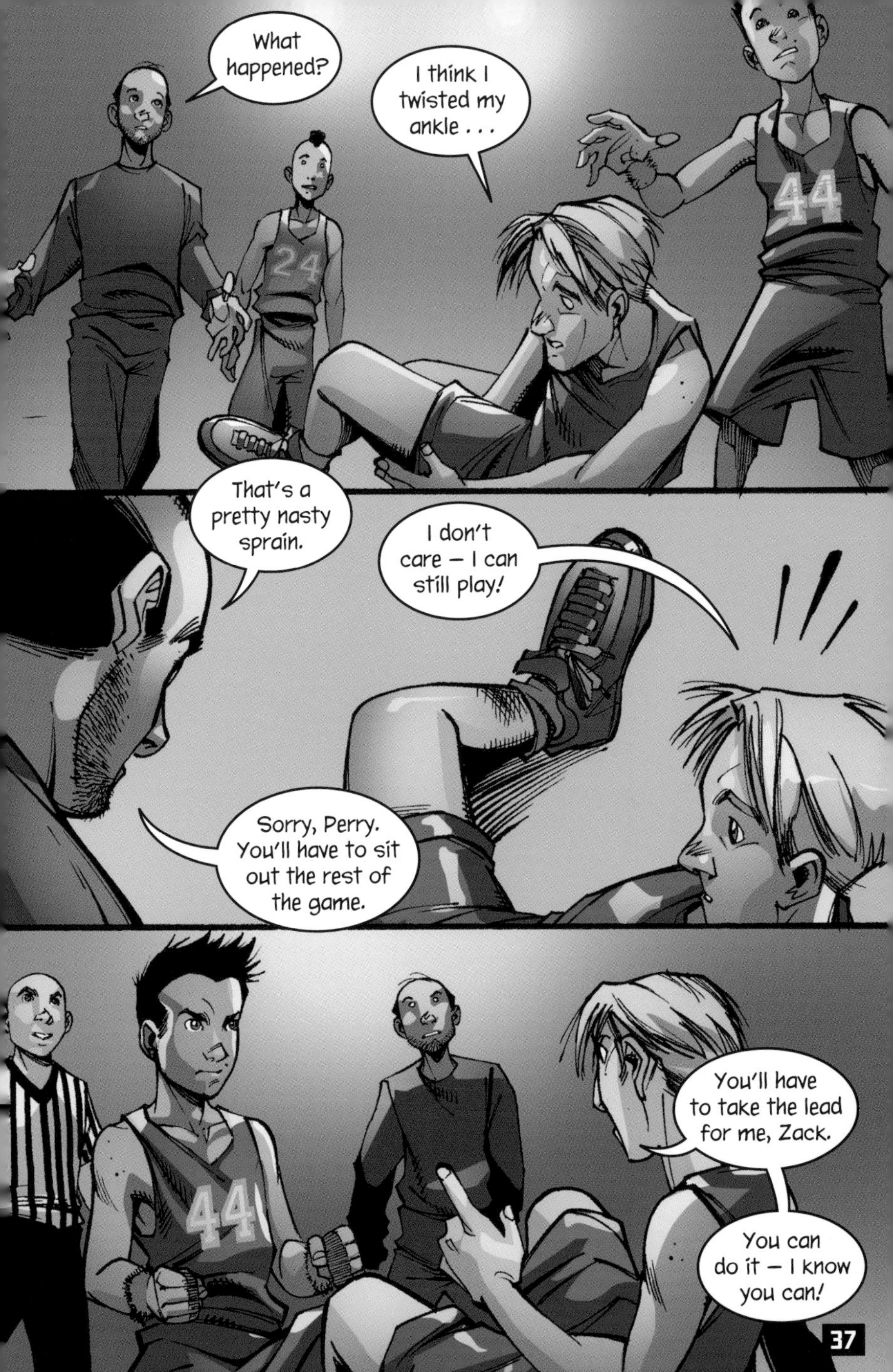
What happened?
I think I twisted my ankle . . .
That's a pretty nasty sprain.
I don't care — I can still play!
Sorry, Perry. You'll have to sit out the rest of the game.
You'll have to take the lead for me, Zack.
You can do it — I know you can!

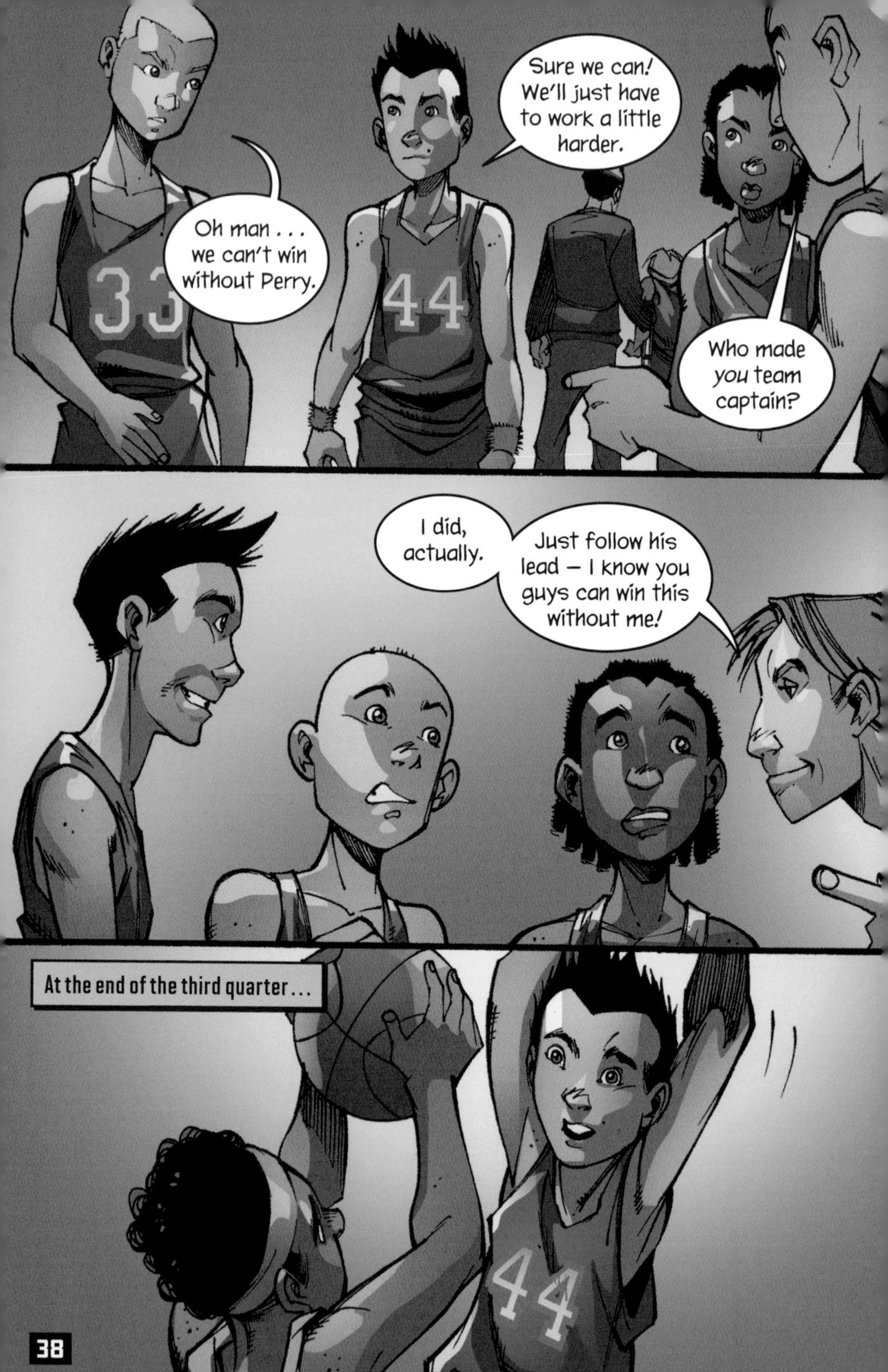
Oh man . . . we can't win without Perry.
Sure we can! We'll just have to work a little harder.
Who made *you* team captain?
I did, actually.
Just follow his lead — I know you guys can win this without me!
At the end of the third quarter . . .

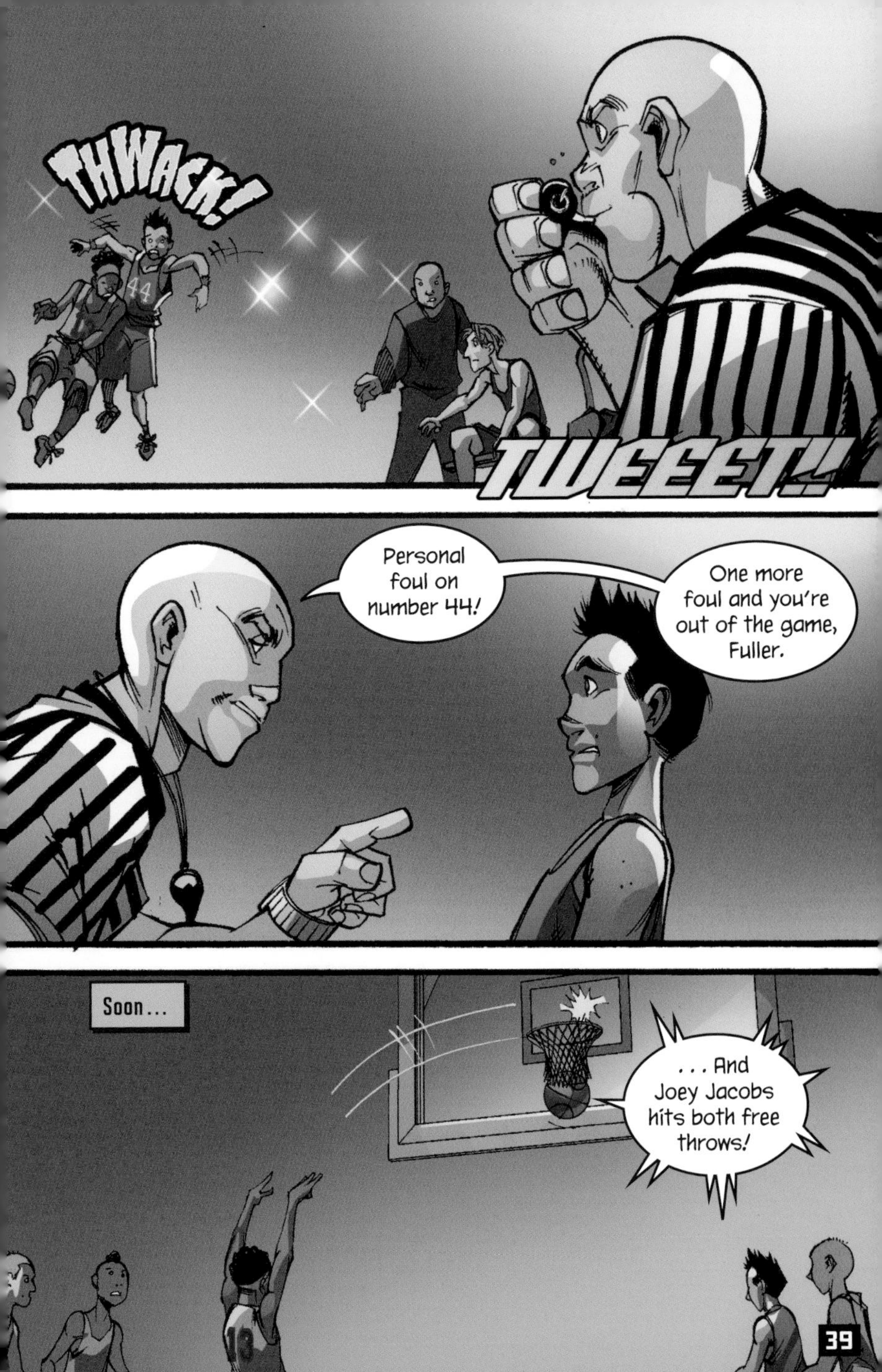
THWACK!
TWEEET!!
Personal foul on number 44!
One more foul and you're out of the game, Fuller.
Soon...
... And Joey Jacobs hits both free throws!

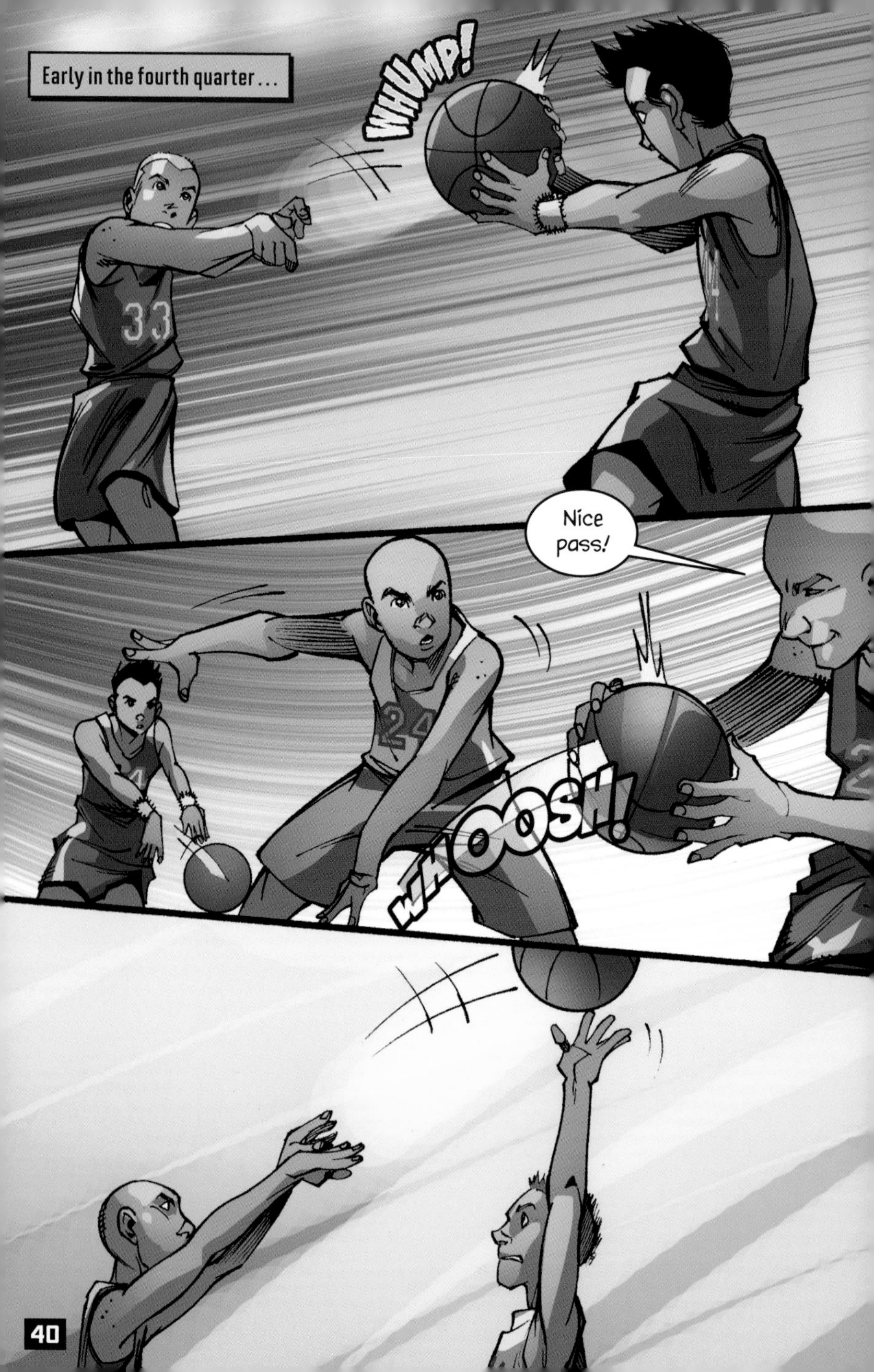

Early in the fourth quarter . . .
WHUMP!
Nice pass!
WHOOSH!

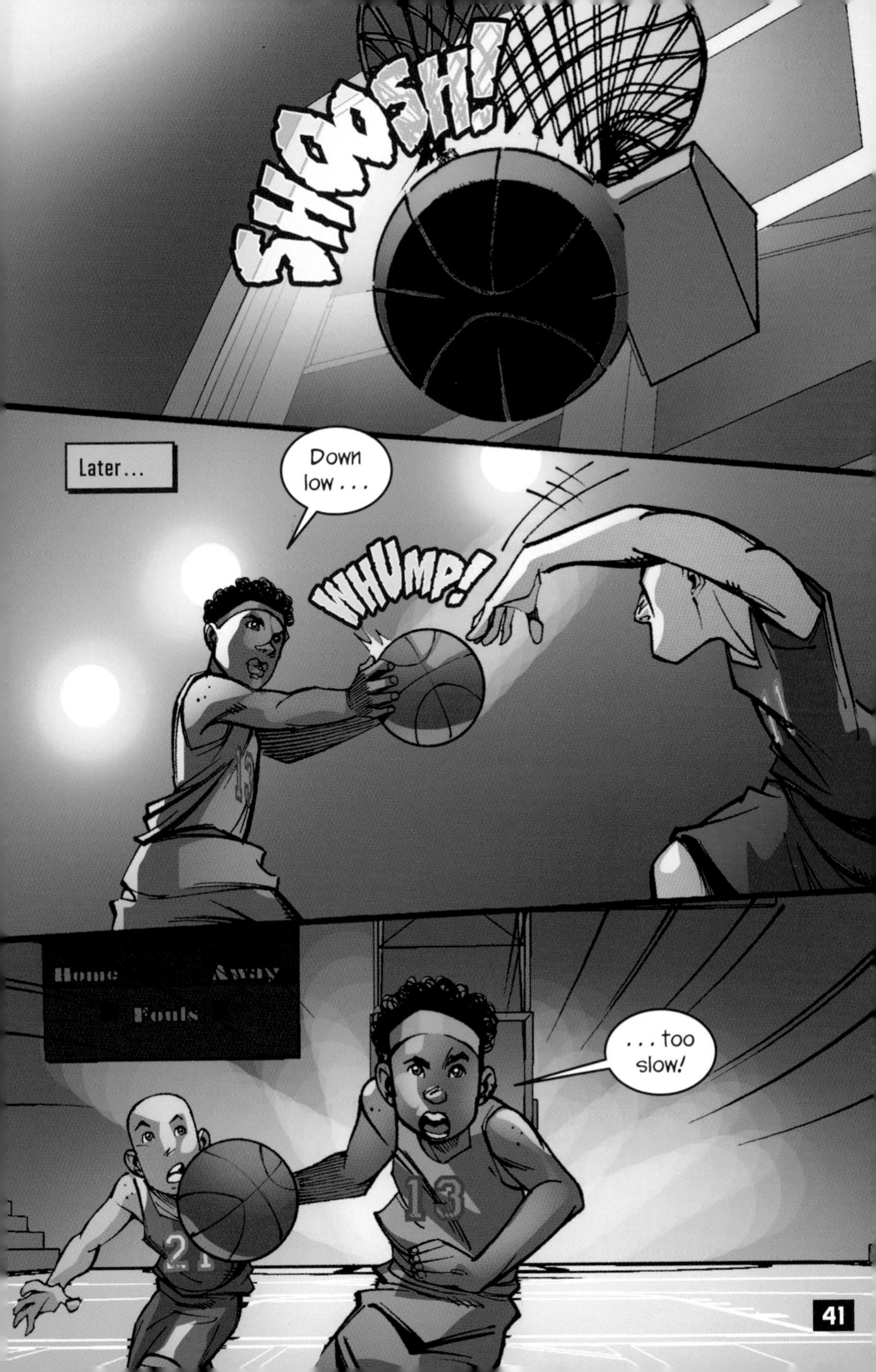
SHOOSH!
Later...
Down low . . .
WHUMP!
Home
Away
Fouls
. . . too slow!

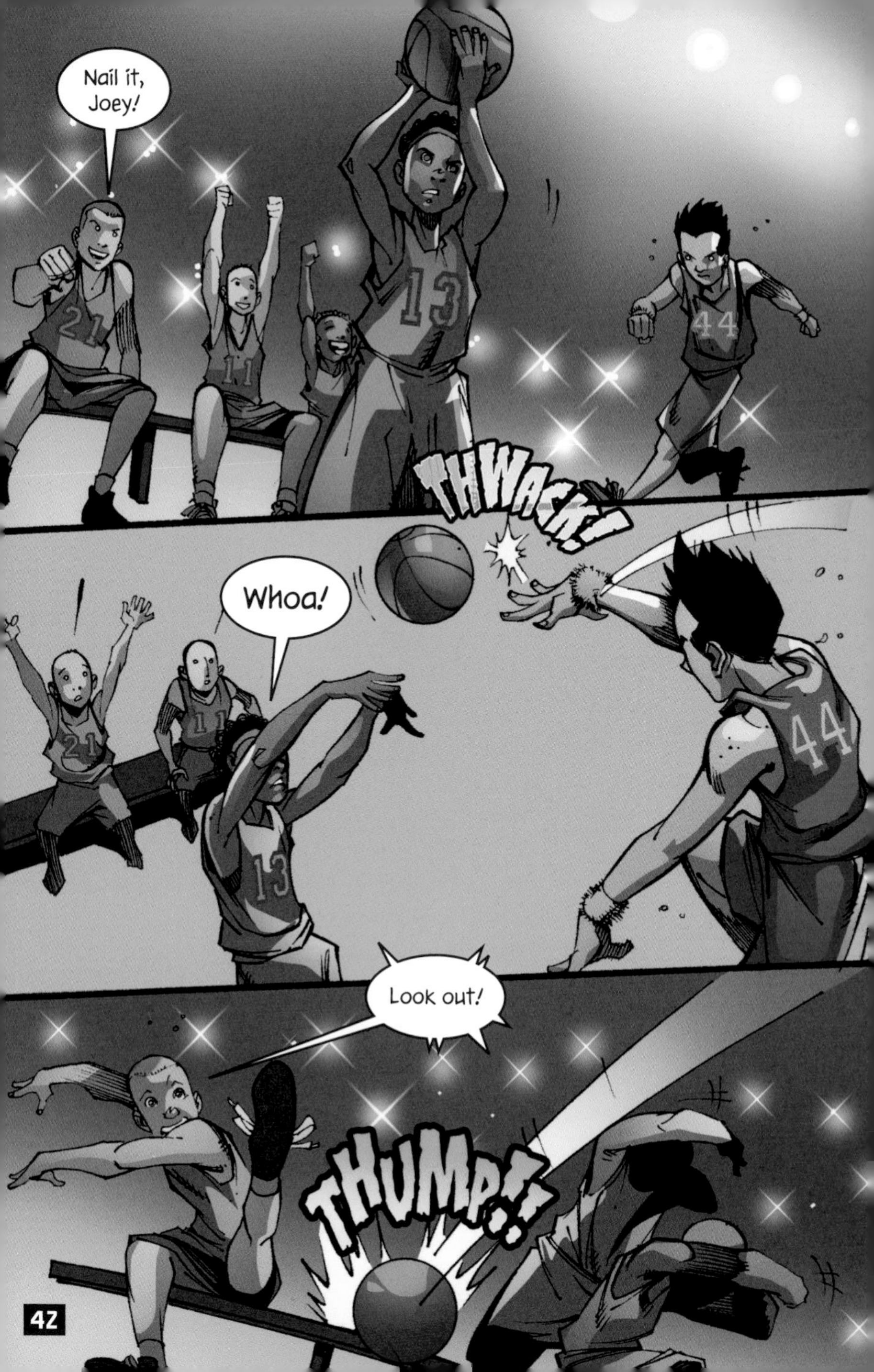
Nail it, Joey!
THWACK!
Whoa!
Look out!
THUMP!!

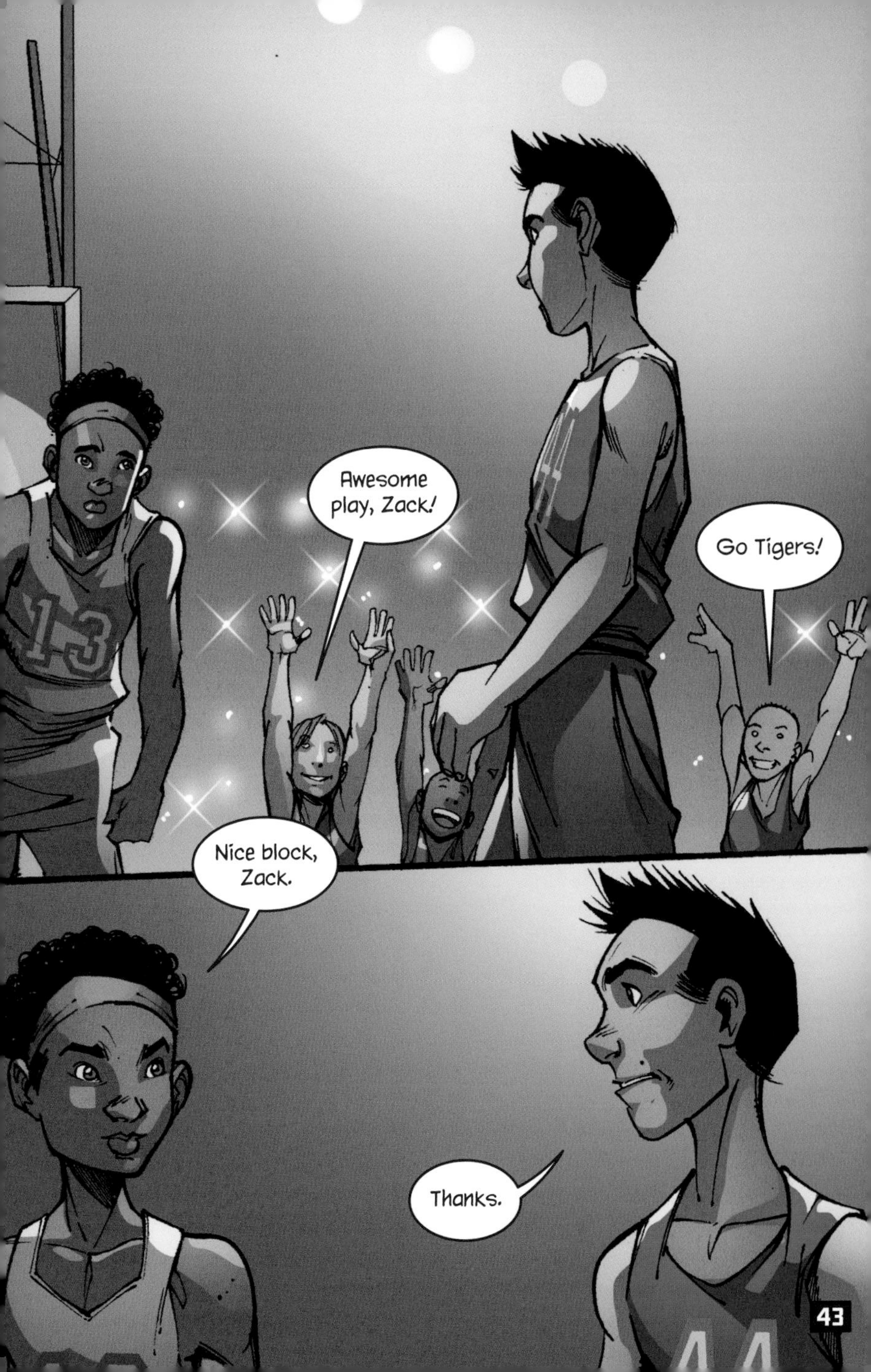

Awesome play, Zack!
Go Tigers!
Nice block, Zack.
Thanks.

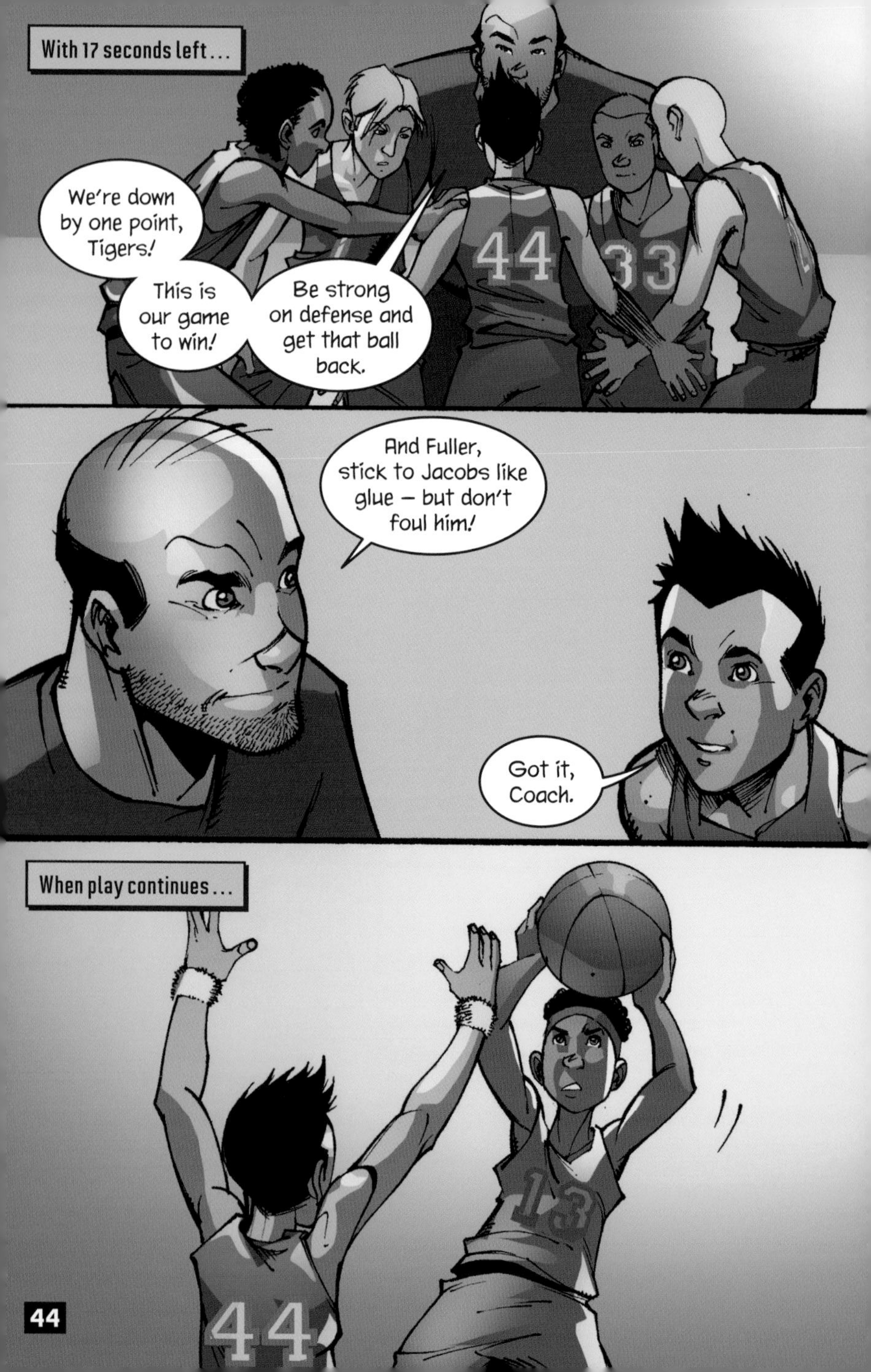
With 17 seconds left . . .
We're down by one point, Tigers!
This is our game to win!
Be strong on defense and get that ball back.
And Fuller, stick to Jacobs like glue — but don't foul him!
Got it, Coach.
When play continues . . .

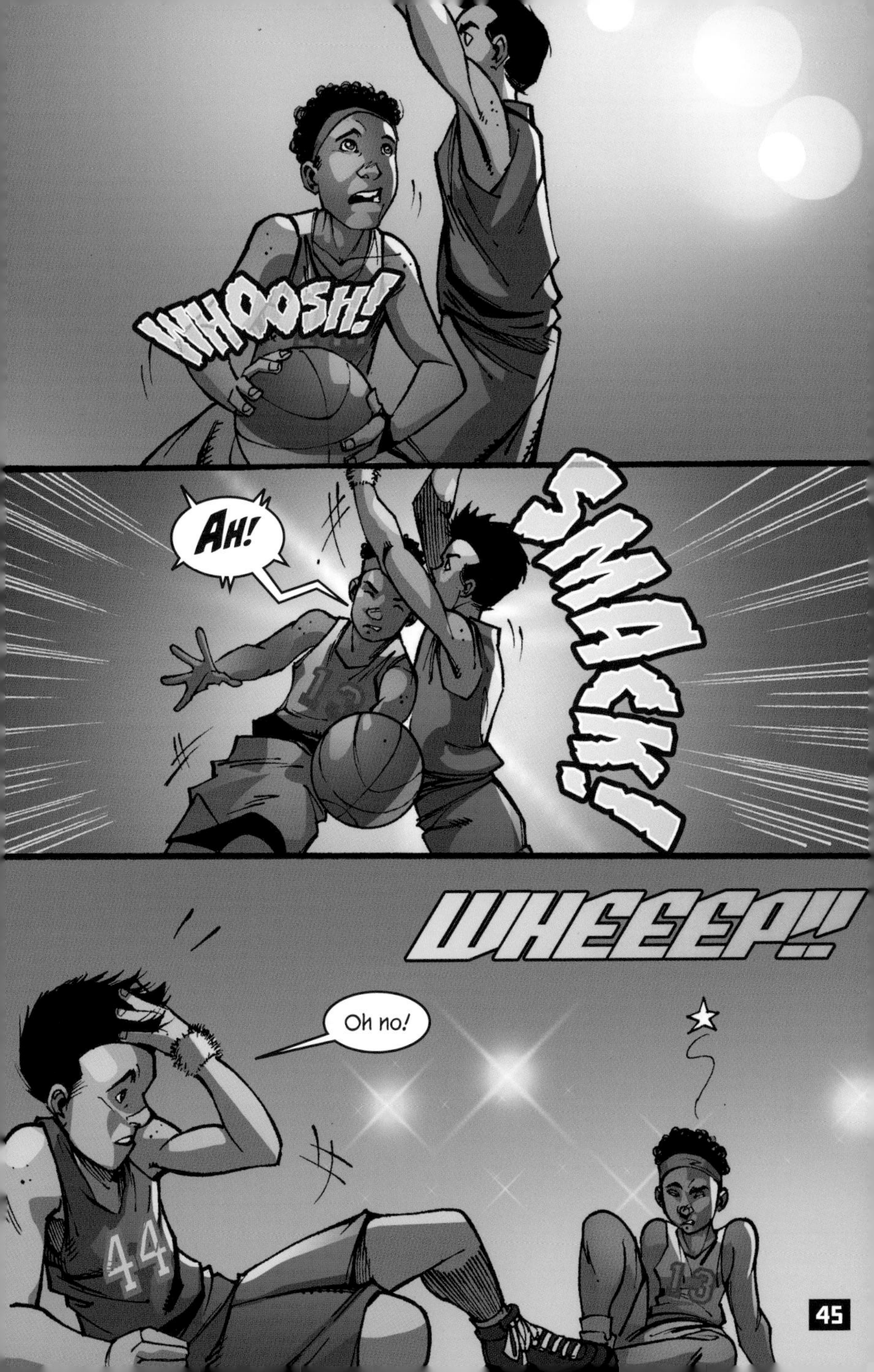
WHOOSH!
AH!
SMACK!
WHEEEP!!
Oh no!

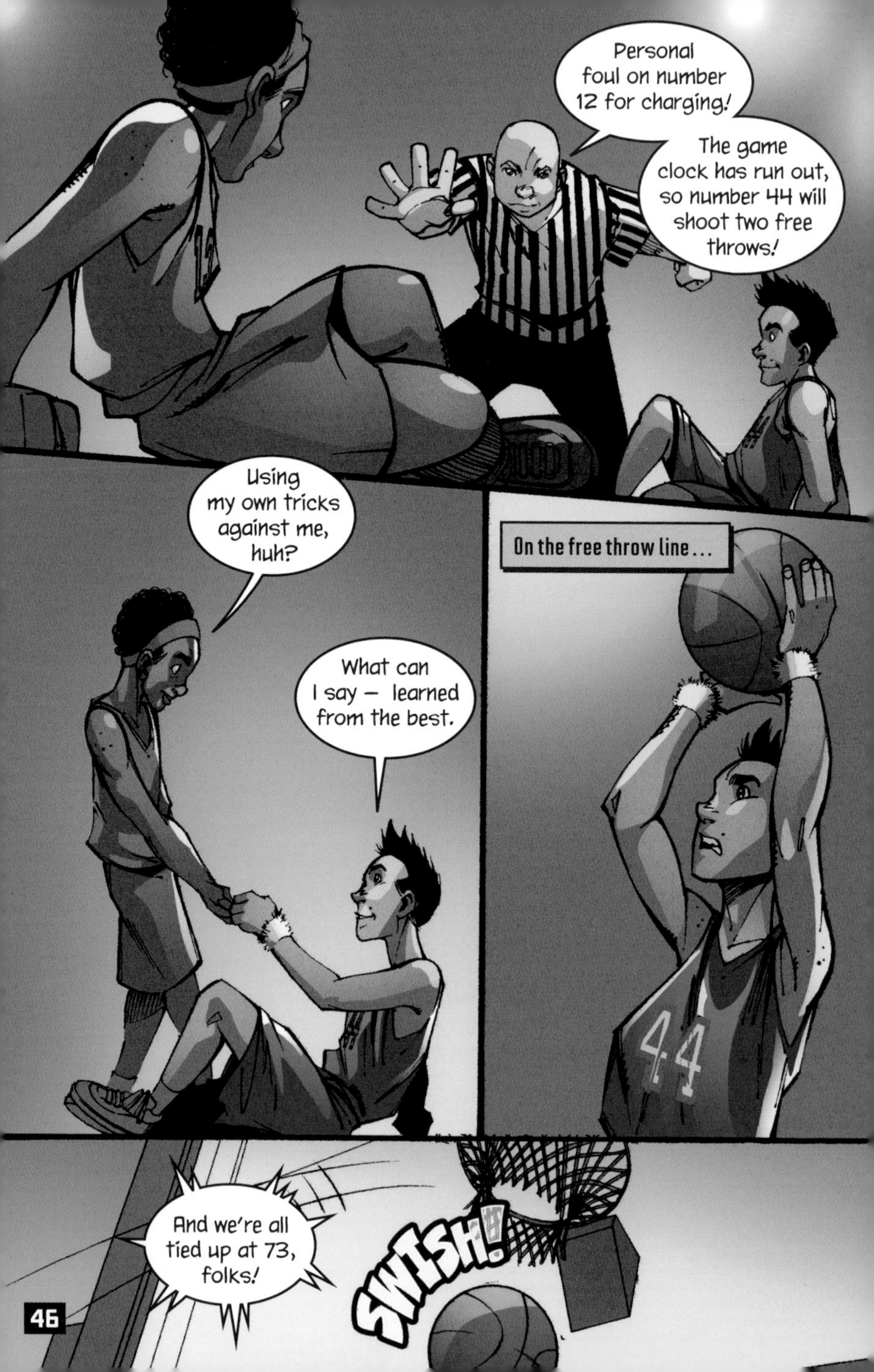
Personal foul on number 12 for charging!
The game clock has run out, so number 44 will shoot two free throws!
Using my own tricks against me, huh?
What can I say — learned from the best.
On the free throw line . . .
And we're all tied up at 73, folks!
SWISH!

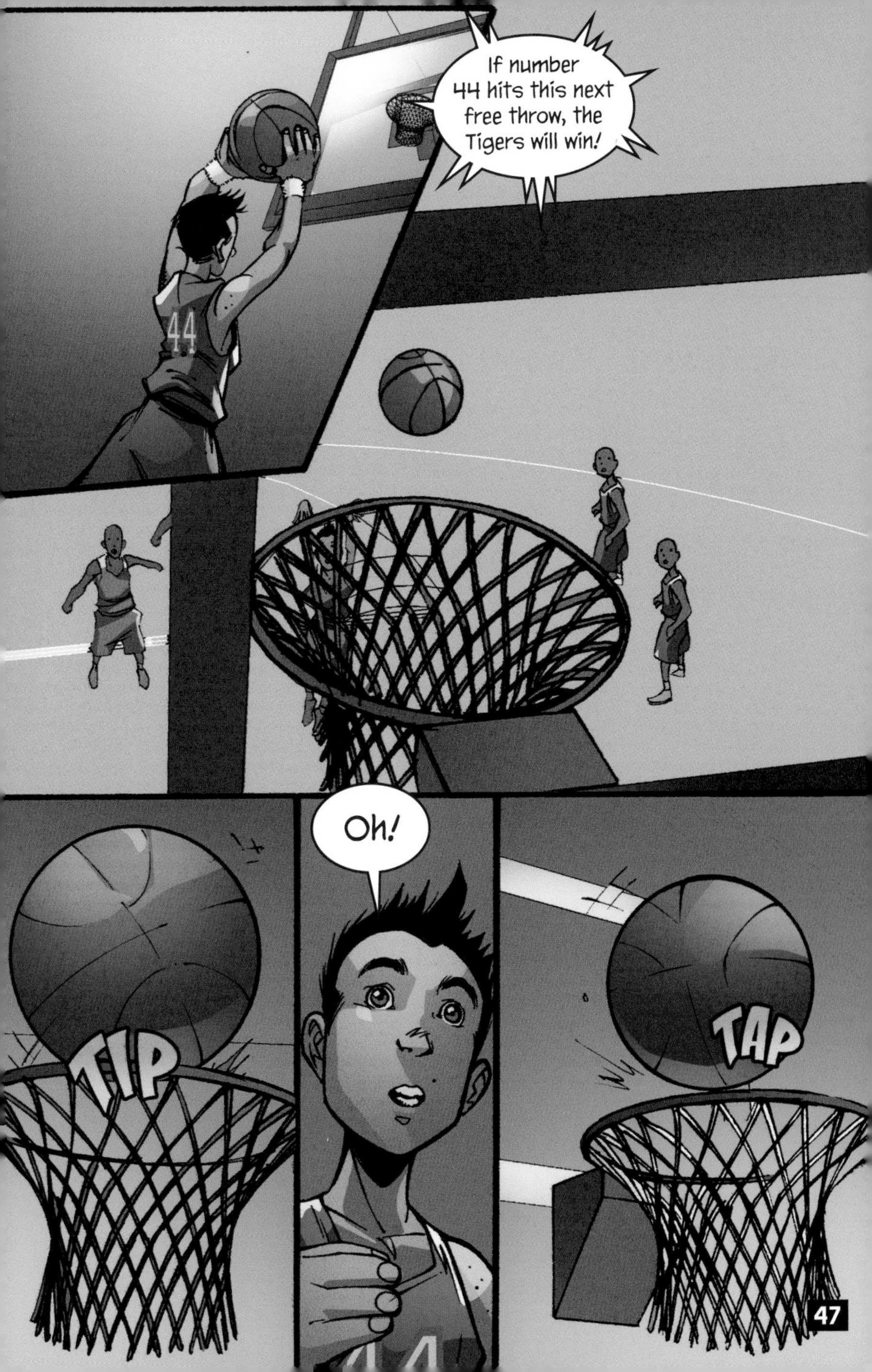
If number 44 hits this next free throw, the Tigers will win!
TIP
Oh!
TAP

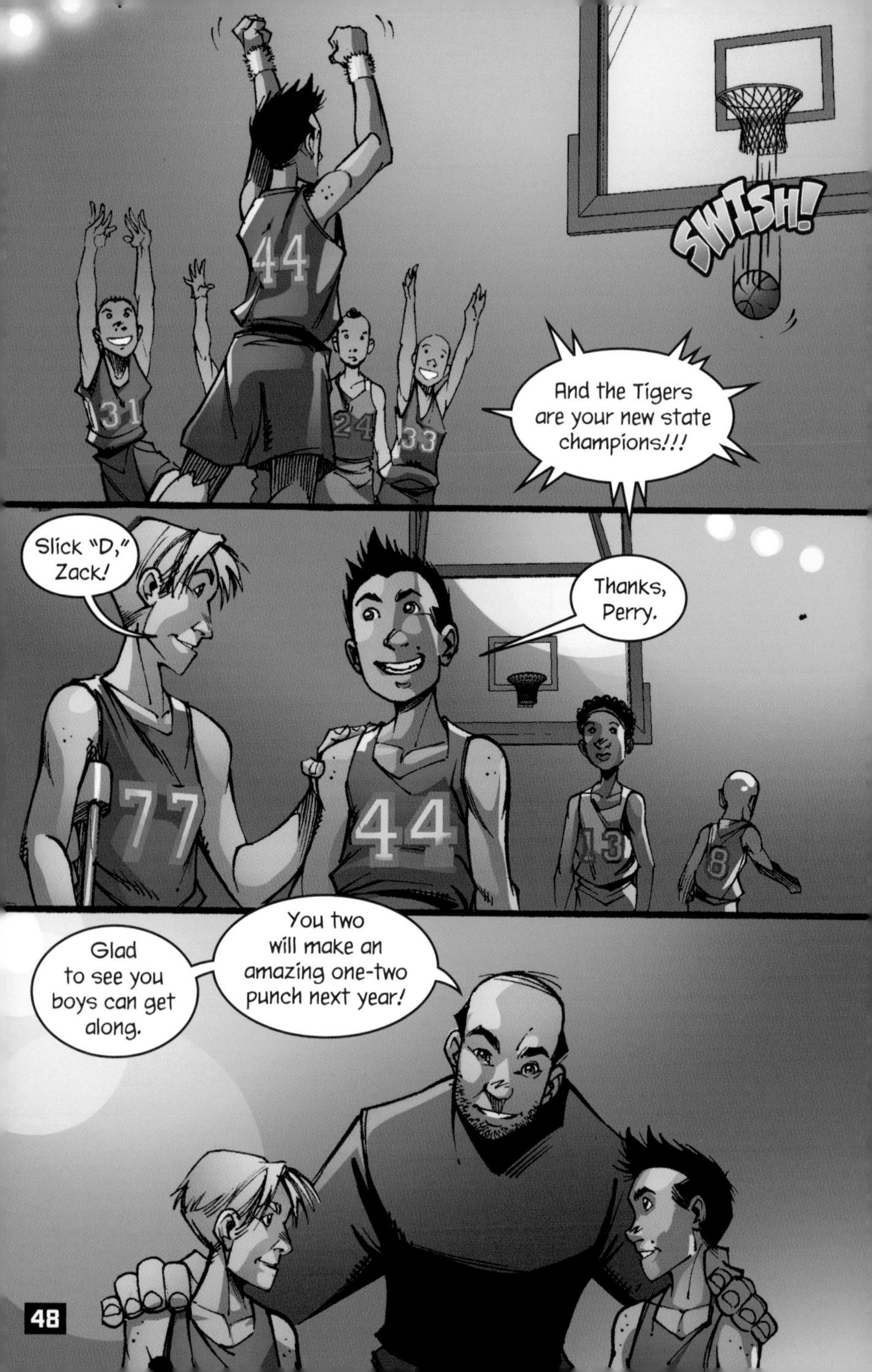
SWISH!
And the Tigers are your new state champions!!!
Slick "D," Zack!
Thanks, Perry.
Glad to see you boys can get along.
You two will make an amazing one-two punch next year!

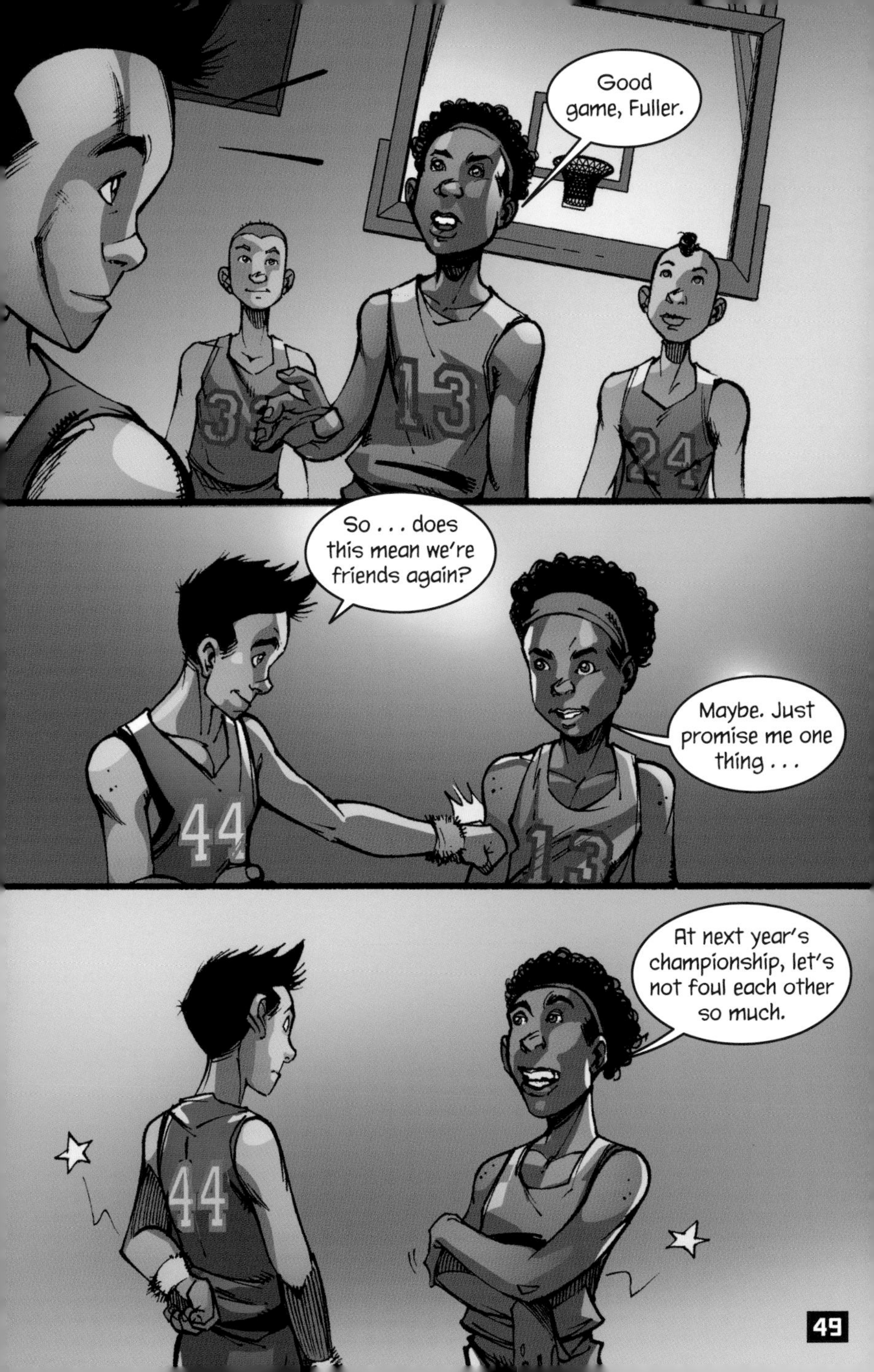
Good game, Fuller.
So . . . does this mean we're friends again?
Maybe. Just promise me one thing . . .
At next year's championship, let's not foul each other so much.

PORTS ZONE

STGAME RECAP

L
LL

FULLER

TIGERS

FULLER OVERCOMES FOUL TROUBLE TO WIN STATE TITLE FOR TIGERS!

44
31
24
33

Y THE UMBERS

NAL SCORE:
GERS: 74
ULLDOGS: 73

AME HIGHS:
OINTS: BOYD, 22
OULS: FULLER, 4
LOCKS: FULLER, 5

STORY:
Zack Fuller survived early foul trouble to score the game-winning free throws after time had expired. The win gives the Tigers their first ever state title. Team captain, Perry Boyd, was quoted as saying, “Zack really stepped up his game today. We couldn’t have won without him.”

Sports Illustrated KIDS

UP NEXT: SI KIDS INFO CENTER

SZ POSTGAME EXTRA

WHERE *YOU* ANALYZE THE GAME!

BLZ vs BHS
3-1
TGR vs ROR
33-32
EAG vs BAN
14-7
SPA vs WLD
4-3
BAN vs ROR
21-15
ROR vs LIG
4-3
BLZ vs
3-1

Basketball fans witnessed an exciting game today when Zack clinched the win for the Tigers from the free-throw line. Let's go into the stands and ask some fans for their thoughts on the day's events...

DISCUSSION QUESTION 1

Zack has to compete against his best friend, Joey Jacobs. Have you ever competed against a friend? Can opponents also be friends with each other?

DISCUSSION QUESTION 2

Zack had to transfer to a new school after his family moved. Was it fair for Joey Jacobs to be angry at Zack for switching schools? Why or why not?

WRITING PROMPT 1

Perry Boyd injures his ankle during the big game. Have you ever gotten injured? What were you doing when it happened? Write about it.

WRITING PROMPT 2

Zack wins the big game for the Tigers. Have you ever won a contest or competition? What did you do? How did it make you feel? Write about your experience.

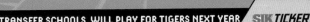

Sports Illustrated KIDS

INFO CENTER

GLOSSARY

ASSET (ASS-et)—something or someone who is helpful or useful

CHARGING (CHAHR-jing)—a foul which occurs when an offensive player runs into a defender who has established position

FORMER (FOR-mur)—previous or earlier

HEAD-FAKE (HED-FAYK)—a faked shot attempt used to trick a defending player into thinking a shot is coming

RUIN (ROO-in)—to spoil or destroy something completely

THREAT (THRET)—a warning that punishment or harm will follow if a certain thing is done or not done

TRAITOR (TRAY-tur)—someone who betrays a friend, team, or trust

CREATORS

JESSICA GUNDERSON › *Author*

Jessica Gunderson grew up in North Dakota. She is currently a writer and teacher in Madison, Wisconsin, where she lives with her husband and her cat.

ALFONSO RUIZ › *Illustrator*

Alfonso Ruiz was born in Macuspana, Tabasco in Mexico, where the temperature is just as hot as the sauce is. He became a comic book illustrator when he was 17 years old, and has worked on many graphic novels since then. Alfonso has illustrated several English graphic novels, including retellings of Dracula and Pinocchio.

JORGE GONZALEZ › *Colorist*

Jorge Gonzalez was born in Monterrey, Mexico. Jorge began his career as a colorist for the graphic novel retellings of *The Time Machine* and *Journey to the Center of the Earth*. In 2006, Jorge, along with several other artists, established Protobunker Studio, where he currently works as a colorist.

Sports Illustrated KIDS GRAPHIC NOVELS

QUICK COMIC

TOU YANG AND DARREN BROODY IN:

KICKOFF BLITZ

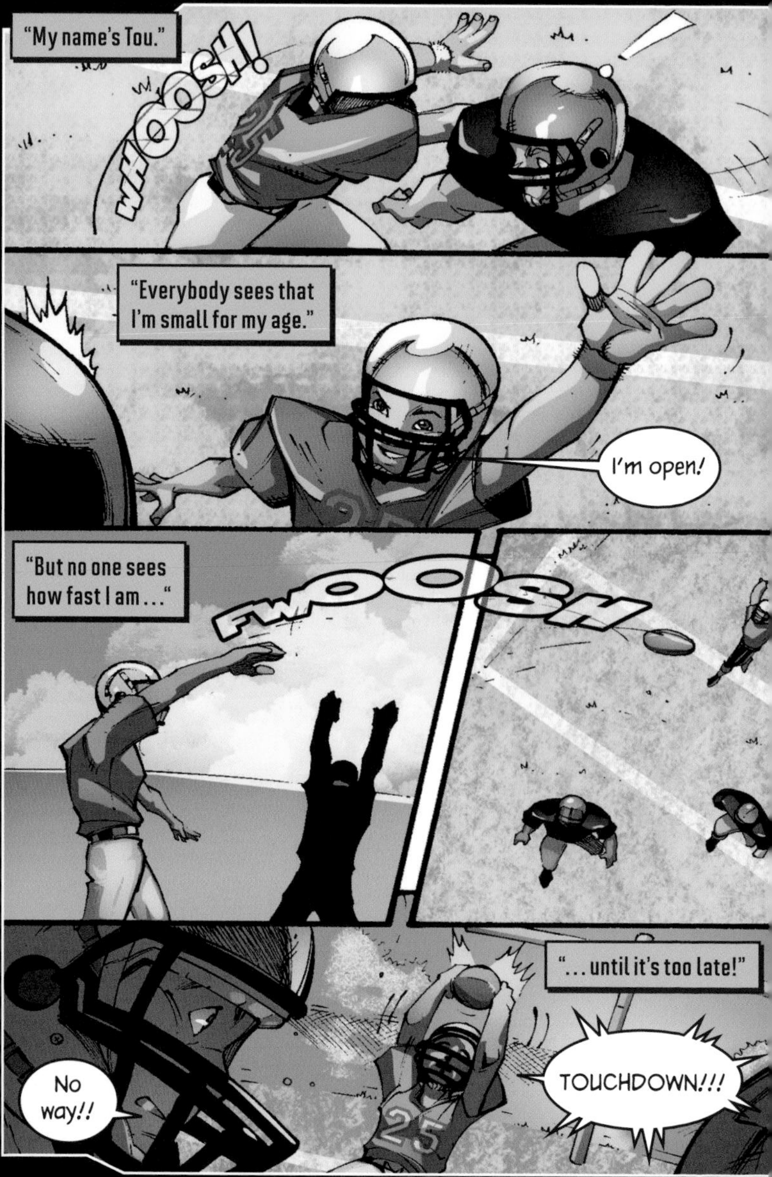
"My name's Tou."
WHOOSH!
"Everybody sees that I'm small for my age."
I'm open!
"But no one sees how fast I am..."
FWOOOSH
"...until it's too late!"
No way!!
TOUCHDOWN!!!

LOVE THIS QUICK COMIC? READ THE WHOLE STORY IN KICKOFF BLITZ – ONLY FROM STONE ARCH BOOKS!